Only an idiot  **he stubborn sc**

And maybe Fran_____ng?
This was no rom_____n.
Not that roman_____y. Every
man had deficienc_____ _nd that happened to be his.

Realizing she hadn't budged from her precarious spot on the edge of the slope, he cursed. He had to get her down. "What are you waiting for?"

"For hell to freeze over!" she yelled back in a very unladylike manner.

"Consider it frozen! Don't make me come up there, C.J., or so help me—"

"What? What is it you'll do to me?"

He heard the panic in her voice, and thought quickly of how he could defuse it. "I'll kiss you again! Only I won't stop there—I'll touch you in places you didn't know you had. Before I'm through, you'll be begging me to make love to you!"

Dear Harlequin Intrigue Reader,

What's bigger than Texas…? Montana! This month, Harlequin Intrigue takes you deep undercover to the offices of MONTANA CONFIDENTIAL. You loved the series when it first premiered in the Lone Star State, so we've created a brand-new set of sexy cowboy agents for you farther north in Big Sky country. Patricia Rosemoor gets things started in *Someone To Protect Her*. Three more installments follow—and I can assure you, you won't want to miss one!

Amanda Stevens concludes her dramatic EDEN'S CHILDREN miniseries with *The Forgiven*. All comes full circle in this redemptive story that reunites mother and child.

What would you do if your "wife" came back from the dead? Look for *In His Wife's Name* for the answer. In a very compelling scenario, Joyce Sullivan explores the consequences of a hidden identity and a desperate search for the truth.

Rounding out the month is the companion story to Harper Allen's miniseries THE AVENGERS. *Sullivan's Last Stand*, like its counterpart *Guarding Jane Doe*, is a deeply emotional story about a soldier of fortune and his dedication to duty. Be sure to pick up both titles by this exceptional new author.

Cowboys, cops—action, drama…it's just another month of terrific romantic suspense from Harlequin Intrigue.

Happy reading!

Sincerely,

Denise O'Sullivan
Associate Senior Editor
Harlequin Intrigue

P.S. Be sure to watch for the next title in Rebecca York's 43 LIGHT STREET trilogy, MINE TO KEEP, available in October.

SOMEONE TO PROTECT HER

PATRICIA ROSEMOOR

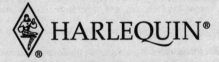

TORONTO • NEW YORK • LONDON
AMSTERDAM • PARIS • SYDNEY • HAMBURG
STOCKHOLM • ATHENS • TOKYO • MILAN • MADRID
PRAGUE • WARSAW • BUDAPEST • AUCKLAND

Special thanks and acknowledgment are given to Patricia Rosemoor for her contribution to the MONTANA CONFIDENTIAL series.

ISBN 0-373-22629-2

SOMEONE TO PROTECT HER

ABOUT THE AUTHOR

Patricia Rosemoor is the recipient of the 1997 Career Achievement Award in Romantic Suspense from *Romantic Times Magazine*. To research her novels, Patricia is willing to swim with dolphins, round up mustangs or howl with wolves.... "Whatever it takes to write a credible tale." She even went to jail for a day—as a guest of Cook County—to research a proposal. Ms. Rosemoor holds a Master of Television degree and a B.A. degree in American literature from the University of Illinois. She lives in Chicago with her husband, Edward, and their three cats.

Books by Patricia Rosemoor

HARLEQUIN INTRIGUE

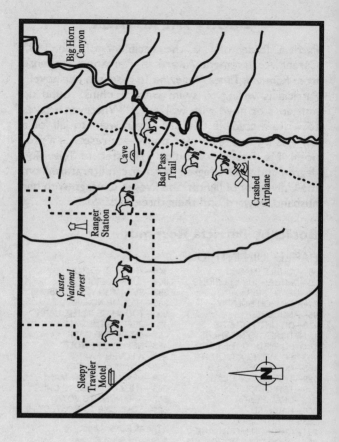

Big Horn Canyon

Cave

Bad Pass Trail

Crashed Airplane

Ranger Station

Custer National Forest

Sleepy Traveler Motel

N

CAST OF CHARACTERS

Frank Connolly—The former military pilot vows to protect his charge with his life.

C. J. Birch—The brilliant scientist is knowledgeable about everything but men.

Gilad—The mercenary's mission is to convert or kill C.J. His reputation is on the line, and he has never failed yet.

Jewel McMurty—The adolescent experiences the pangs of first love for Frank.

Daniel Austin—The Montana Confidential team leader is faced with stopping danger from several directions at once.

Knowing nothing about planes, flying
or transporting horses by air when I started this book,
I must give credit to those who gave me the information
I needed to select the correct plane that could
both transport horses and land in the mountains
and to write a realistic controlled crash.

Thanks to writers Vickie Spears, Cassandra Blizzard,
Mary Adamski and Harriet Robbins Ackert.
To pilot Clifford Wells and his wife, D.J.
And to horse transporter Carl Webster.

Prologue

The photograph didn't do her justice.

He studied the woman hiding behind the too-big lab coat and glasses. Innocent and unsuspecting, she was standing before the building nestled into the Rocky Mountain foothills, shading her eyes against the brilliant Colorado sun as if she were looking for someone.

Him?

He imagined her letting go of her too-obvious inhibitions, letting down her hair and begging him to thread his fingers through the honey-blond strands. He could almost see her throwing back her head and arching her long, elegant throat in invitation.

He chuckled…merely a way to amuse himself while waiting. Nothing got in the way of business—neither the job he was being paid for or his own agenda.

He ran a forefinger over the photograph. "The subject is in view."

"She doesn't see you watching her, does she?" came the hollow voice through his headset.

Keeping himself from turning off the cell phone clipped to his belt in irritated response, he clenched his jaw and said, "I'm invisible."

"Invisible" being one of his specialties, the reason he had been hired.

At the moment, he was camouflaged behind the handicapped card dangling from his rearview mirror. Physically fit people avoided looking at those with disabilities, as if the condition were contagious. And the card was his invitation to a parking spot right near the entrance of the National Center for Aquatic Research, where British scientist C. J. Birch worked.

For the moment, anyway.

"What is she doing?"

Other than taking a candy bar from her pocket and breaking off a chunk of chocolate?

"Leaving the premises, I assume."

"Well, don't let her get away!"

Watching the chocolate disappear into her full, unpainted mouth made him stir in his seat.

He could take her here. Now. Right from under the noses of the unsuspecting employees who threaded the grounds. But that might call attention to himself, the last thing he wanted.

Besides, he had a personal debt to collect and this situation would give him the opportunity for which he'd been waiting.

Two men, also in lab coats, exited the building and stopped to talk to the woman. Had she been waiting for them? It seemed so when they all started for the parking lot together.

"She won't get away from me," he murmured more to himself than to his contact. "She's not alone now, but I'll find the right moment to get to her and soon."

"*How* soon—"

"I'll let you know when I have her."

Ripping the headset from his ears, he turned off the

cell phone and cut the connection before the impatient man could make any more ridiculous demands.

He turned the key in the ignition. The engine hummed to life and his vehicle quietly slid from its spot to stalk her.

The woman was walking with the men and yet not, he noticed. She kept to one side of the pair and left a gap that bespoke volumes about her comfort zone with the opposite sex. An incentive—like any predator, he enjoyed playing with his prey before consuming it.

He was a professional, hired but not hurting for money, not needing the work. What he needed—demanded—was stimulation. Excitement. A challenge. Something clever to add to the mystique of his reputation.

He never duplicated a job.

Never failed, either.

Never.

Chapter One

"Gran told me you're originally from South Dakota, not Montana. How come you didn't say so? What about your family?" Jewel McMurty asked in her rapid-fire style. "You don't have a wife and kids, do you?"

The twelve-year-old's bright green eyes pinned Frank Connolly as he washed the dust from a chestnut quarter horse named Sierra Sunrise, who'd topped his racing career at more than a million dollars in winnings. Now the lucky devil would be standing at stud, getting his chance with a different vixen or two on a daily basis.

"Just a brother. He's the one with the wife and kids. And his own ranch."

"So why aren't you there?"

"Got a job to do." Ostensibly to work with the horses on Lonesome Pony, though his real job as a Montana Confidential agent was equally vital and a lot more dangerous. He'd barely had time to stow his gear before he was put to work when he'd arrived several days before. "Which you're keeping me from doing."

Lonesome Pony. He knew all about being lonesome. Figured the girl did, too. Her parents were divorced, and she'd been bundled off to live with her grandparents for a while—no one her own age to hang with. Desperate for attention, she'd been following him around like a lost puppy ever since he'd arrived, and he hadn't been hardhearted enough to discourage her. Like all kids, she had a million questions, mostly personal, mostly about the past he didn't want to talk about. Damned if he'd be telling her his sob story. He didn't want to think about Bosnia, no less share the nightmare with a kid.

He gave Jewel a playful squirt with the hose. While she shrieked with laughter, she stayed put.

"I can help, you know."

"These boys think they're hot stuff," Frank said, indicating the trio of stallions that had been delivered barely an hour before. "I wouldn't want a little thing like you to get trampled."

"Little?" All gangly limbs, she drew herself up as tall as she could and still missed the five-foot mark. "I'm nearly a woman!"

Thinking she'd be insulted if any laughter dared escape his lips, Frank bit the inside of his cheek. "You could do me a big favor, then."

"What?" she asked, young voice ripe with suspicion.

"Take care of Silver over there."

He indicated the pasture across from the main house, where an old gelding that had been sent over from a nearby spread stared out at the action he couldn't join.

He looked lonesome, too.

"Yeah, I saw him come in this morning," Jewel said. "Why is he all by himself? And how come he limps? What's wrong with him?"

"He got hit by a truck on a ranch road a while back. This here's gonna be his retirement range."

"Hit by a truck?" Jewel's expression went solemn. "He's going to be okay, though, right?"

As okay as a thirty-year-old, badly injured horse could be, Frank thought.

What he said was, "He'll always have that bum hip. Can't keep up with his pals, so he could use some human attention—lots of good grooming, tasty treats and smooth talk. You up to that?"

Jewel nodded and eyed the mottled white horse. "I'm very reliable. Ask Gran or Gramps. They'll tell you."

Gran and Gramps were Dale and Patrick McMurty, the elderly caretakers who lived in the main house with Daniel Austin, head of operations for Montana Confidential. Dale cooked and kept house, while Patrick was a crack handyman.

Patrick also happened to be a retired military man who knew how to keep his own counsel about what really was going on underground at Lonesome Pony— that the ranch was a cover for Montana Confidential, a division of the Department of Public Safety.

Frank dug into a pocket and pulled out a plastic bag filled with apple chunks. Sierra Sunrise nosed his arm and Frank slipped him a treat. He stored a few pieces in a vest pocket and held out the bag.

"You can start with these."

Jewel's smile was brilliant. Snatching the offering from his hand as eagerly as had the stallion, she whipped around, her long blond ponytail bobbing.

And, now uninterrupted, Frank quickly went to work. The horses enjoyed the spray of water and soapy scrub. And they didn't refuse the apple chunks he'd kept back for them. He always carried treats when working around horses. And being big-money boys, these stallions were used to lots of pampering and attention.

He wondered if they'd miss the track. They'd spent their young lives running fast, being caught in the limelight. He knew a little about that, too. But he'd gladly left the limelight to others—so maybe the boys would feel the same.

Besides, Frank thought, catching sight of a pretty golden mare nosing her way through the slats of the pasture fence, they had compensations. The soft-eyed mare peered out at them and whickered flirtatiously. The stallions snorted and stomped and did their best to look studly in return. Frank grinned. The mating dance had begun. Slipping the boys into their own individual paddocks outside the barn, he checked his watch—just about time for the meeting.

Awaiting him was the fancy log house with its wide porch overlooking the pasture, and beyond that, the mountains. He could get used to living in Yellowstone country with its spectacular alpine scenery. The Absaroka-Beartooth Wilderness lay to the east, the foothills of the Gallatins to the west. A man couldn't ask for a prettier home.

Or a more unusual one.

Lonesome Pony had been a guest ranch for decades—hence a bunch of rifle and archery ranges and horseshoe pits plus a fancy circular corral for those former Friday night rodeos still lined the fine-gravel walk between the house and barn. On the other side of the property, a hut well-stocked with gear stood near the bend in Crooked Creek, which provided some of the most spectacular fly-fishing in the country. But the

oddest thing to Frank was the swimming pool surrounded by cabins, providing separate living quarters
for him and the other agents.

At least he would have his privacy, something he
treasured after months of enforced communal living in
a stinking hole.

Ahead, the McMurtys stood in the small garden to
one side of the house.

Wisps of thinning white hair sticking out from the
brimmed hat pulled low over his sun-leathered face,
Patrick dumped a sack onto the ground. "Are you
gonna stand there so you can tell me every move to
make, woman?"

"Only if I want you to get it right the first time,"
Dale said, fists on her ample hips.

"If you don't like the way I do things—"

"I know. Do it myself. But if I don't participate,
you'll think I'm ignoring you."

"We could try it that way and see for sure," Patrick
suggested slyly.

Frank figured they'd keep things lively for his
boss—if they didn't drive the man crazy with their
bickering.

Dale spotted Frank. "I don't know why I've put up
with this old buzzard for nearly forty years. He can't
keep a civil tongue around me."

Patrick mimicked her. "If I did, you'd think I was
ignoring you."

"Sounds to me like true love," Frank said, pushing
back painful memories of his own.

Before the McMurtys could respond, a shrill voice
came from the other direction. "No, Daddy! No!"

Carrying his cranky daughter from the cabin area,
Kyle Foster, one of the other agents, spoke to her in a

low, soothing voice. "Mrs. Mac is going to take good care of you for just a little while."

The blond moppet screwed up her face and began to wail "Da-a-a-d-dy!" as she fisted his shirt. She looked so fragile pressed against her father's broad, solid frame.

"Shh, honey. You be a big girl and I'll let you ride your pony later. You want to ride Ribbons, don't you?"

Molly rubbed her eyes with balled fists. Even to an old bachelor like Frank, it was evident the three-year-old needed a nap. He caught Kyle's attention and indicated he was heading for the house. Looking as if he were about to tear out his sandy brown hair, Kyle nodded.

"You take a nice nap for me," Dale chimed in, "and when you wake up, I'll have some homemade oatmeal cookies with lots of raisins for you."

Frank didn't know if it was the promise of the pony ride or the cookies that sealed the deal, but Molly finally allowed the housekeeper to take her from her father. Kyle caught up to him at the long porch that fronted the main house.

"I don't know if I was cut out for this—not the job, but being a single father."

"Being a responsible parent takes more work than any profession, that's for certain. But I'm sure you'll get the hang of it."

Frank knew all about Kyle Foster, bomb specialist. He'd been a hero until a bomb scare had gone wrong and his partner had died in the explosion. Guilt had plummeted Kyle out of the L.A. force, but law enforcement was obviously in his blood, for he hadn't resisted Daniel's recruiting tactics. Frank didn't envy Kyle's having to balance a dangerous job with parental responsibilities, but, unfortunately, his wife had left him no choice when she'd dumped her child as well as her husband for a Hollywood film producer.

They entered the house. The big open living area bespoke its past as "Dude Ranch Meeting Central."

The former lounge and lobby rose two stories, as did the massive fireplace constructed from local river rock. A moose head balefully looked down at them through glass eyes. Over the middle of the room hung a chandelier of elk horn. And a cast-iron bighorn sheep challenged them from the windowed area where Daniel stood, back to them, phone to his ear.

"Yeah, Mitch, so far, so good. The locals don't suspect anything."

Frank knew Daniel was talking to Mitchell Forbes, who had run the Texas Confidential operation. Daniel had worked as an agent there, and though he had retired from active duty, he'd been asked to start a branch of the agency in Montana where a serious terrorist threat had the Department of Public Safety worried.

"They just figure I'm a crazy man for wanting to become a rancher at my age in this economic climate. They treat me with friendly tolerance." Daniel turned and silently greeted his two agents. He indicated he'd only be a minute. "Uh-huh."

Frank threw himself onto one of the club chairs upholstered in a Navajo pattern and appreciatively gazed at the framed photographs lining the opposite wall—a turn-of-the-century chronicle of the railroad, rodeos and roundups of the area.

"I'm not looking forward to baby-sitting her, that's for certain," Daniel was saying. "I'm only doing it as a favor to the director. Listen. Frank and Kyle are here, and I want to meet with them, fill them in and make sure that we have what we need."

The Montana Confidential operation was just getting off the ground. So far, the men had been busy building their cover. Frank didn't mind working with the horses—a side benefit of the job, actually—but he was eager for an assignment.

When Daniel hung up, Frank asked, "So who are you baby-sitting?"

"Whitney MacNair."

"Of the Washington and Martha's Vineyard MacNairs?" Kyle asked.

The nation's second family of American politics, Frank knew. As a MacNair, Whitney had grown up privileged and pampered and in the spotlight. Her face was better-known to him than any cover girl's.

"The same," Daniel agreed. "Her family was furious when the press ran with the story about her accepting gifts from her boss and they quickly yanked her out of the limelight."

Her boss being the very married Senator Ross Weston. Frank mused, "Odd that she's being sent here, to Weston's home state."

"Her father asked the Director of the Department of Public Safety for a favor, and since I needed an assistant…" Daniel ran a hand through his blond hair and shrugged. "We'll make it work somehow. Weston's not from these parts, anyhow, so I don't imagine him showing up on our doorstep anytime soon. Now, gentlemen, let's get down to business."

"Down" being a secret room built below the study.

They followed Daniel into a room off the main living area. It appeared to be a typical if spacious office with a computer desk and seating area and a spectacular view of the mountains. The walls were lined with built-in bookshelves. Daniel went to an inner wall and reached behind a book of Montana photographs. A click and the section of bookshelf swung open.

"Gentlemen..."

Frank led the way into an elevator car, Kyle following, Daniel bringing up the rear. He slid the bookshelf unit back in place and hit the down button. The machinery no more than whispered its presence as the car descended to the secret "war" room below.

"I haven't even had time to check out the equipment," Daniel said. "I'm sure we'll have to shake out some bugs in the system before we're operating smoothly."

Computers, fax machines and telephones awaited in the communications center. The men split up and for the next hour or so thoroughly checked out the electronics.

Frank put one of the computers through its paces. Once satisfied all was as it should be, he left the area to check out the rest of the quarters. Locked cabinets—weapons and ammunition—lined one of the low-ceilinged walls. Another work area held listening devices and cameras. He noted a red warning light perched over a nearby closed door. Lab for surveillance photography, he guessed. They had everything they would need to do their jobs and then some.

Daniel and Kyle caught up with him; they took seats around a large conference table where materials were already laid out. Enough for four men, Frank noted, when only the three of them were present.

He asked, "So are we it for now?"

"For however long it is until Special Agent Court Brody arrives," Daniel agreed.

"FBI," Kyle muttered. "Suit-and-tie law enforcement. Yeah, he'll blend in with the locals, all right."

"Actually, he'll blend better than any of us." At the far end of the table, Daniel fiddled with what looked to be one of several dossiers spread out in front of him. "Brody grew up in this neck of the mountains—a positive for us. And he's only on loan from the FBI until I can recruit another permanent agent."

"As long as he doesn't think he's in charge and doesn't get in our way," Frank said.

He had no fondness for special agents, not after the Bosnia debriefing.

"Don't worry, I'll do my best to stay out of your way."

As one, all three men at the table turned toward the deep voice coming from the other side of the room.

Speaking of the devil...

Court Brody had sneaked up on them all. He stood at the elevator, arms crossed over his chest, eyes hidden by sunglasses undoubtedly meant to intimidate.

Daniel cleared his throat and stood. "Come in, come in. We're just getting to know one another."

"So I heard."

Frank watched the big man—tall, rather than wide—stalk them. He didn't seem too happy.

Well, neither was Frank.

He felt flushed and outside of himself. What the hell was wrong with him? Hadn't he learned to be on guard at all times? The elevator operated almost silently, true, but what had happened to his instincts?

Without instincts, in a combat situation, a man could be dead in the blink of an eye.

A rush of adrenaline exacerbated the pounding of Frank's heart. It pounded so loud the sound filled his ears. Surely they could all hear it. He glanced around the table, but no one was paying him any mind.

Daniel and Kyle were focused on the FBI man, who took the end seat as far from them all as he could. Only then did he remove the sunglasses to reveal cold gray eyes. If he and Kyle didn't welcome Brody...well, the feeling was too obviously returned.

"Welcome to Montana Confidential." Daniel returned to his seat and made formal introductions. "Court Brody, special agent, FBI. Frank Connolly, pilot and ex-military man. Kyle Foster, chemist and former member of the L.A. bomb squad." He took a big breath and paused, but no one else spoke. "Well, I hope you're all ready to get to work."

"Horses or otherwise?" Court drawled.

Daniel smiled in the face of the man's tightly held hostility. "This morning I received information that members of a terrorist group called the Black Order have been slipping into Montana via the Canadian border."

Court appeared skeptical. "To what end?"

"Rumor says they want to get their hands on a new biological weapon—D-5, a water-borne virus."

"To what end?" Court asked again.

"We don't know yet, but if they succeed and get it into a major water supply, it could mean big trouble for a lot of folks."

Frank jumped in before Court could hold center stage. "D-5?" He'd heard about the virus. As far as he knew, "big trouble" spelled death. "Where?"

"The Quinlan Research Institute. Scientists there are working on an antidote, so they have a quantity of the virus, of course."

"And without the D-5 at the lab, there will be no

antidote,'' Kyle said. ''How close are they to developing one?''

''Not even in the ballpark. That's why we're bringing in British scientist C. J. Birch from the National Center for Aquatic Research.'' Daniel turned his gaze to Frank. ''Rather, you are as soon as we're finished here. The ranch plane is online, waiting for you at the Boulder Municipal Airport.''

''What about a first officer?'' Frank asked. The plane was a twin-engine DC-3, requiring two in the cockpit.

''Rent-a-pilot by the name of John Vasquez. He'll meet you at the field tomorrow morning. Your cover is that you're picking up some prize quarter horse mares for the ranch's breeding program. But your real mission is getting C. J. Birch to the Quinlan Research Institute tomorrow, safely and without drawing too much attention.''

Frank didn't voice the opinion that flying in horses would raise more than a few eyebrows. Normally the only horses transported by air rather than truck were Thoroughbreds being ferried from Europe or Japan or the Middle East, or across country to big-money races.

But rather than a fancy jet, they would use a reconditioned pre-World War II DC-3. The old tail-draggers were workhorses—no pun intended—usually put to use these days hauling cargo that didn't move around, hence the need to palletize the horses.

The plane itself wouldn't draw too much attention, especially since it would land on a runway already laid out on Lonesome Pony land. Lots of the bigger ranches had their own planes, Frank knew, if normally single-prop jobs. And he guessed if the locals heard about the horses, that would merely serve as proof of Daniel Austin's madness in setting up what was sure to be a money-losing breeding ranch.

But back to the operation and the reason the scientist needed to be brought in undercover. "You're expecting trouble?" Sweat trickled down Frank's spine at the thought.

"Hopefully not, but just in case, I want Birch protected by the best."

Which wasn't necessarily him, Frank feared, though he kept his mouth shut on that score. Too late to raise questions about his capabilities at this point. He'd already committed himself.

But question himself he did as Daniel wrapped up the meeting and sent him off to pack an overnight bag before being driven to the Bozeman airport, where a charter would get him to Boulder before dark. Was he ready to be responsible for another's life? Or had he been a fool to let Daniel sweet-talk him into Montana Confidential?

Truth was…he just didn't know.

He only knew he had to prove himself. To make up for what he'd been unable to stop from happening…to make amends, somehow.

Maybe then the nightmares would quit him.

As the agents left the house, a dark green SUV pulled up with a screech of tires. A woman with red-gold hair slid out from behind the wheel. The moment her high-heel-clad feet touched the gravel, Frank recognized Whitney MacNair.

She pushed down her designer sunglasses and murmured, "Just what I need, some hunky men."

Opening the back of the SUV, she revealed a pile of designer luggage. She turned her gaze on Frank.

"Sorry, ma'am, I already have an assignment."

Undaunted, she walked right up to Court and slipped a hand around one arm. "Ooh, so strong," she cooed. "And I can tell you're a *real* gentleman."

Frank kept going, glancing over his shoulder to watch the show. It did his heart good to see a scowling Court Brody be forced to haul the woman's luggage inside.

Frank's log cabin was the farthest from the swimming pool. The most isolated, the reason he'd chosen it. The living area, bedroom and bath all had been decorated by the same hand as had done the main house. Some would consider these to be small quarters, but after the hellhole that had been home for five months, Frank considered them palatial.

Quickly gathering a few articles of clothing and throwing them into an overnight bag, he set it next to the rucksack he never traveled without. Then he grabbed his Stetson, left the cabin and wended his way around the swimming pool. Waiting next to the ranch truck, Patrick McMurty was talking to Daniel and Kyle.

As he caught up to the men, Whitney stuck her head out a second-floor window. "Excuse me, but I'm desperate. I need some more muscle up here...to move the furniture around. If I'm going to be happy living here, then I need to mix things up a little."

Frank figured she was going to mix things up a lot.

"Damn, we don't have time for such nonsense," Daniel muttered.

As if she expected the objection, Whitney pulled a helpless expression. "Pretty please."

Kyle muttered, "She doesn't seem like the kind to give up."

"Yeah, yeah. And we wouldn't want her to be unhappy.'' Daniel held his hand out to Frank for a brisk shake. ''Good luck. We'll see you and Birch tomorrow.''

''Tomorrow,'' Frank echoed as Daniel and Kyle rushed off.

Glad for his excuse to get out of dancing to the woman's tune, Frank shook his head and climbed into the passenger seat.

Already behind the wheel, Patrick started the truck. ''That one's gonna be something else.''

''Daniel can handle her.''

Patrick shot the truck down the driveway, spewing gravel in all directions. Frank felt himself hurtling toward a situation that could too easily spin out of his control.

Suddenly, getting to know the lovely, if spoiled, Whitney MacNair seemed far more appealing than going after some nerdy little man who could be a powder keg in disguise.

CECILIA JANE BIRCH wasn't thrilled to be leaving for the wilds of Montana at the crack of dawn the next morning. Having lived her entire thirty years in ultracivilized England but for the past few months, she considered Boulder, Colorado, as uncivilized as she cared to get. All those mountains in the distance...all that open sky...all those snakes, one of them with her name, she was certain.

She shivered at the thought.

But her work was her life, after all, and the Quinlan Research Institute needed her expertise, so she had no choice, really.

And how much less civilized could things get, anyway?

At least that's what she decided to believe as she left her colleagues to their drinks at the outdoor table of the Brickwalk Café, where they'd had a dinner meeting to catch up loose threads. Not knowing how long she might be gone, she'd turned over her files to her assistant Len Miller, who would take over the project she'd been heading—for good if he had anything to say about it, she assumed.

Well, it just couldn't be helped.

Dusk had fallen over the Pearl Street Mall, the red-bricked pedestrian-only heart and soul of the city. The area around the restaurant was sparsely populated since an outdoor concert with Cowboy Sam and the Spurs had lured university students to the other end of the mall. Now, if only they knew some civilized tunes. C.J. had always preferred the classics.

She did enjoy the short walk along historic buildings housing numerous shops, galleries, offices and sidewalk cafés—not that it could compete with London, of course. All summer, entertainers had abounded, including the Zip Code Man, who could identify towns and sometimes even describe building styles in neighborhoods, based on a visitor's zip code. Then there was the sword swallower, contortionist, juggler and professional accordionist—all buskers who played for the hat.

As she stopped to pull a chocolate bar from her pocket, a sudden goosey feeling along her neck gave her pause. Surreptitiously, she looked around.

From a few feet away, a bronzed statue seemed to be watching her.

C.J. blinked. Not a statue, but another busker, skin and clothing like painted bronze. He leaned on his closed umbrella, his hat upended at his feet. Then he deliberately changed positions to a new pose and froze.

Performance art such as this she would never understand, C.J. thought, caught by the statue's steady gaze on her as she backed off.

For some reason her mouth went dry and she realized she was holding her breath.

Suddenly the statue lunged for her, grabbed her arm so that she dropped her candy bar, and whirled her from the walkway toward a side street. Not knowing whether to laugh or to express outrage, C.J. attempted to be good-natured about the situation...until she realized the man wasn't letting up.

"I say, you may stop now!"

But he didn't.

Heart fluttering, C.J. dug in her heels and attempted to pry the man's fingers from her arm. "Sir! What do you think you're about?"

He wasn't letting her go, that was for certain. Not even looking at her, he was inching her into the shadows, away from any conceivable assistance.

"Stop!" she yelled, attempting to hit at him.

Her fist glanced off his arm, not deterring him in the least, so C.J. did the only thing she could think of—she opened her mouth and screamed. Quite loudly. Before she could see if anyone noticed, her attacker jerked her and knocked the breath from her. She threw herself to the ground. He barely paused before continuing to drag her.

"Stop, please!" she gasped out as her hip hit a bump in the walkway. "Take my wallet and leave me be."

He didn't so much as pause.

Frantic now—what did he want if not her money and credit cards?—C.J. tried grabbing on to a litter can, but she couldn't get ahold before he jerked her along. Her shoulder burned viciously. She cried out again, but had little hope that anyone would hear.

"What is it that you want?" she cried, fearing the worst.

Her very life?

shaking, horror-stricken. "Be careful!" she finally
managed after everyone was quiet.

"I want to thank you, ma'am," she said to Verna
finally.

Chapter Two

Wondering if she would be alive to see the sunrise,
C.J. was amazed when a man hurtled past her and tack-
led the busker so hard the force almost ripped her arm
from its socket before the knave finally freed her.

A panting, hurting, horribly frightened C.J. tried to
make out the identity of her rescuer, but it was nearly
dark now. All she could see was a tangle of limbs as
the men did a bizarre dance away from her seemingly
in slow motion. Punches were traded, though in such
close quarters, she suspected neither man had enough
leverage to do harm. Suddenly, her attacker forced the
other man away from him, kicked out and connected
with the man's knee, then ran, so the incident was over
nearly as quickly as it had begun.

Her rescuer caught himself and appeared ready to
follow the blackguard, but then he stopped and limped
back to where she still sat in a dazed puddle.

"Are you all right?"

"Yes—at least I think so." Testing her limbs, she
winced when she stretched out her abused arm.
"Bruises and strains, I suspect, but I shall live. Thanks
to you."

"Let me help you up."

The touch of his strong hands at her waist shot a foreign sensation through C.J. He helped her to her feet and continued to steady her. Inches from her attractive dark-haired savior—she could see that much, at least— she felt her throat clog. That darned tongue of hers must have swollen to twice its size as it often did around interesting men. And when he reached out to right her glasses, which sat crookedly on her nose, her knees weakened.

"Can you walk?" he asked.

Glad for the excuse to put some distance between them, she nodded her head and demonstrated. The joints wobbled but worked. Well, perhaps it was more of a teeter than a true walk, but she managed.

When a few yards separated them, she choked out, "You see? All better."

"But I can't just leave you here." He looked past her. "Think you can make another half block?" He indicated the hotel ahead. "I can get you there, make sure you're safe until someone can come for you."

She nodded, not bothering to protest that there would be no one to fetch her. No husband. No suitor. Not even a female friend, since she hadn't been in the country long enough to bond with anyone. But a respite in soothing surroundings was the very thing, she decided. He took her arm in a gentlemanly fashion and let her set the pace.

Realizing that he was still limping slightly, she said, "Perhaps it's you who is hurt."

"Nah, just an old war injury kicking up."

Humor? she wondered. At a time like this? How curious. As they approached the old hotel that had been restored to its former elegance, his stride evened out, so she didn't think more of it.

C.J. loved Hotel Boulderado with its domed, stained-glass skylight, cantilevered oak staircase and lovely period furniture. In addition to eating in the hotel's restaurant, she often wandered through the place and sat in the lobby as if waiting for a friend, when all she wanted was to experience the pleasure of being in someplace civilized.

Upon entering, she found a chair in a corner, "Oh, yes, this is better."

The man's brow furrowed. "You're a Brit. Odd…"

"Yes, I'm surprised to find myself in your Wild West, as well," she agreed, a sense of euphoria filling her. The aftermath of the adrenaline rush of being attacked, she was certain.

"No, it's just that I was looking for this British scientist when I saw that guy dragging you off."

Scientist? C.J. gaped. How many British scientists could be working in Boulder, Colorado?

The man sat in a chair that brought their knees close, making her shift in her seat away from him.

"We really should report this incident to the police." He rubbed the back of his neck. "But I need to find this guy tonight."

"I believe you have. C. J. Birch here." She extended her hand.

His piercing blue eyes widened on her. "You're…?"

"Exactly. And you?"

He gave her hand a vitally American shake.

"Frank Connolly, Montana Confidential. I'm flying you out of here tomorrow."

Noting that he hadn't let go of her hand, C.J. murmured, "How bizarre."

"What?"

She slipped from his grasp and stared at her fingers for a moment. Then she blinked and looked at him. "Why, the way you found me, of course."

"I was told you would be having a dinner meeting at the Brickwalk Café. But when I got there...one of your colleagues told me you'd just set off."

"Perfect timing, then." As if fate had taken a hand and stepped in to protect her. Making C.J. feel a bit better about her coming circumstances. "Well, I'm settled down inside now, so perhaps we should make that report to the authorities."

"No!" Frank followed the loud retort by scanning the lobby.

C.J. followed suit. No one seemed to have noticed.

"No authorities?" she asked. "Why not?"

"Considering who you are...who I am...it complicates matters."

Her turn to go wide-eyed. "You think the attack had something to do with my work?"

Frank continued peering around the lobby, as if he were now looking for suspects. "Possibly."

That thought had never entered her mind. "Then the local authorities—"

"Might delay your departure. We can't afford that."

"No, we can't." C.J. had been brought up to speed about the urgency of finding the antidote to D-5. "But what if...if the attacker indeed *was* after *me*. If he could find me on Pearl Street—"

"He'd know where you live," Frank finished for her. "I booked a hotel room for the night, but considering what just happened, I'll be staying at your place. Don't worry, I won't let you out of my sight until I get you to the Quinlan Research Institute."

"I do hope you don't mean that literally," C.J. said,

allowing the starch in her voice to thicken. "I do need a good night's rest. You'll find the couch in the next room close enough."

TOO CLOSE, C.J. AMENDED once she was alone with Frank Connolly. He'd fetched his rental car and had driven her from the hotel to her flat near the university, a one-bedroom in a modest complex filled mostly with grad students who were considerate types. Luckily for her, the place had come furnished, so she hadn't had to hunt for nonexistent domestic skills; rather, she'd moved right in and had gotten down to her work at the lab immediately.

Gripping the bedding for the couch to her chest, she entered the living room, thinking how odd a man's presence in her place seemed.

"I really couldn't tell what he looked like under all that paint, Daniel," Frank was telling his supervisor. "He was a fraction taller than me—probably an even six feet. And he was more muscular."

C.J. gave Frank a surprised once-over. Clothed only in a pair of jeans and a soft, sleeveless white T-shirt, he appeared muscular enough. As a matter of fact, she considered him to be quite perfect.

"Yeah, all right. Tomorrow, then."

Flushing at her uncalled-for thoughts, C.J. quickly turned away and spread a bottom sheet over the couch cushions as Frank hung up. Before she knew what he was about, he was far too close.

"You don't have to do that."

"Yes, I do," she said, keeping focused on the sheet rather than the man. "You're a hero. You deserve a civilized bed…even if it's not really a bed."

"Trust me, I've slept in worse. *Much* worse."

She wondered what "worse" meant. A seedy motel, perhaps?

"Here, let me do that."

He took the top sheet from her hands. At the unexpected touch, she sprang back and watched him work. His precise movements. The strength apparent in the contracting muscles of his arms. The way the trim cut of his short dark brown hair threaded with silver perfectly suited his high forehead and broad cheekbones. He reminded her a little of that actor—George Clooney—only sexier.

"Daniel's putting out feelers on your attacker." He took the blanket from her and snapped it open over the couch. "Gonna try to ID him."

"But without a true description," C.J. mused, "where would he even begin?"

"The MO—uh, modus operandi. This guy was a pro, but pros normally try to blend in, a little hard to do covered in bronze paint. So this one's somewhat unique. Might be easier to tag him than if he'd played it like Joe Regular."

"I see what you mean." She dropped the pillows at one end. "Is there anything I can get you?"

"I'll be fine. Get some rest. We'll be up at the crack of dawn."

"Yes. Thank you." She started for her bedroom door, then hesitated. She turned to find him staring at her. Something about his expression made her falter. Then she moistened her lips and said, "I mean that, Frank Connolly. The 'thank you' part. You really are a hero."

With that she slipped into her bedroom, closed the door, then leaned against the wall, trembling. She lived such a quiet, ordinary life. The last few hours—being attacked and rescued, having a man more handsome than George Clooney not only in her apartment but sleeping on her couch—were sure to stand out in her mind forever.

Quickly she stripped out of the trousers and summer sweater that required a trip to the cleaners. Not until she returned to Boulder, whenever that might be. She passed her already packed medium-size suitcase and shoulder bag on the way to the bathroom.

Standing under the shower longer than she normally would, C.J. hoped the pounding hot water would relieve some of the ache of being dragged by her arm, of having her hip make more contact with the ground than was comfortable. She also hoped the water would relax her enough so that she could fall asleep.

But freshly scrubbed and encased in her favorite satiny pajamas, she still found sleep to be an elusive creature. Thoughts continued to roil through her head as she lay in the silent dark.

The burden of finding an antidote before a water supply could be contaminated with D-5.

The horror of having been attacked.

The discomfort of having her too appealing rescuer mere feet away, separated from her merely by a flimsy—and unlocked—door.

HE WAS HIT.

"Get out! Get out!"

No time to think...eject.

A plume of smoke surrounded him, choking him. The crippled jet veered off, nose down, spinning, its death scream sounding in his head.

Explosion...his ears imploded.

He flew down, wingless, through a momentarily silent world.

A world of jagged peaks and valleys coming closer fast.

The chute shot open behind him. He jerked back. Stomach lurched. Then all righted.

He was coming down...but to what?

The ravaged earth met his feet. The stink of fire burned his nostrils. Folds of material enveloped him, taking him prisoner.

He fought, knowing his very life depended on it....

THUMPING...POUNDING...groaning...

Terrifying noises awakened C.J. from an already restless sleep. Heart lurching, pulse pounding, she sat straight up in bed. An intruder? She groped for the telephone, had the slender receiver in hand before remembering.

Frank Connolly.

Her heart thudded. What was going on in her living room? Was Frank fighting off the intruder once more? Half asleep, he would be vulnerable. He could be dead by the time the authorities arrived.

Dropping the phone and grabbing an empty vase, she flung open the door. Barely able to make out thrashing on the couch in the dark, she yelled, ''Stop that!'' and flew across the room.

''Huh? What's going on?''

The deep-throated grumble replaced the more threatening noises and stopped C.J. dead in her tracks. Closer now, she realized Frank was alone. And asleep. At least he had been until she'd come charging in.

A lamp clicked on. C.J. blinked at the magnificent display of Frank's naked torso, cast in gold from the lamplight. The very breath caught in her throat as she allowed her gaze to explore the planes and angles, the muscular perfection that begged to be touched....

"I must have been dreaming," he mumbled, shifting on the couch so that the sheet dropped lower.

Not seeing a band of white—or any other color—along his hip, she wasn't certain he wore anything beneath.

"Or h-having a n-nightmare." The very thought of a naked man on her couch—especially *this* man—was disconcerting. "I, uh, thought you were in trouble."

"And you were going to save me?"

Frank stared at her somewhat in wonder, as if he were really seeing her for the first time. His expression changed subtly. Heat creeping up her neck, C.J. set the vase on a table and shoved her hands behind her back.

"Tea," she offered in desperation as he continued to pin her with his intense gaze. "I have a calming herbal if you would like to try it."

"Sure. That would be great."

Relieved for the respite from the odd tension he caused in her, she fled to the kitchen.

FRANK HAD PULLED ON a T-shirt and his jeans by the time C.J. returned to the living room.

"This should settle you down," she murmured, placing a tray heavy with a porcelain teapot and cups and saucers on the table before the couch.

"I'm fine."

Not appearing to believe him, she sat down on a chair opposite.

Frank watched closely as she poured the tea. Her hands were graceful, her ringless fingers long, her short nails glossy as if she'd just buffed them. She held out a cup on a saucer, and he suddenly realized the delicate set decorated with flowers and dragons was the only really personal item he'd seen in her apartment.

Even that vase she'd commandeered as an impromptu weapon was colorless, like the rest of the apartment. A furnished rental unit, no doubt. Bland, but easy. Still, he wondered why she'd done nothing to make the place her own. It was devoid of the little things he usually noticed in a woman's place.

"Thanks," he said, adding more sugar than was good for him—at least if he wanted to sleep.

She didn't comment, merely raised one pale eyebrow.

"If you need someone to talk to, I'm available."

"I told you, I'm fine."

"If you say so," she murmured, her voice as soothing as she'd promised the tea would be. She took a sip. "But sometimes talking helps."

"Talking can't change anything, can't bring someone back!" Frank said heatedly before catching himself. "Okay, so what's the giveaway?"

"Other than you scaring me half to death in your sleep? Your eyes. You try to hide it, Frank, but when you're not vigilant, they tell me that you're troubled…haunted by your past."

Certain she didn't know about his background—how could she when she hadn't even known who was coming for her—he said, "Perceptive as well as intelligent and beautiful, huh?"

She blinked at him and he could see that she was thrown. "I'm not beautiful—I'm a scientist."

Frank started. Maybe she didn't get many compliments of that sort, considering she hid behind lab coats and glasses and an unflattering hairstyle. But without the glasses, her hair tousled and brushing her shoulders, C.J. indeed appeared beautiful, if in a starched, stiff-upper-lip kind of way. Her body wasn't encased in a lab coat now. Rather, satiny material drowned her curves. The peach-and-cream stripes of her pajamas complemented her honey-gold hair and flawless ivory complexion.

But again, she seemed to be hiding.

And Frank couldn't help but wonder what he might find under the baggy garments.

Cup halfway to her mouth, C.J. hesitated. Their gazes locked for a moment, and Frank felt as if he'd just caught a doe in his headlights. He watched the subtle change in her expression before she hid that, too.

She took a quick sip of her tea, then rose, snatching up her saucer. "Since you're not inclined to talk, anyway, I'll just finish this in my room."

"Something I didn't say?"

But if his comment amused her, she hid it well.

Spine stiff, C.J. retreated to her bedroom.

"I'd rather not fly with an exhausted pilot, so try to let that tea work its magic on you," she murmured, just before she closed the door.

And locked it. Frank was certain he heard the bolt slide into place.

To lock him out? he wondered.

Or herself in?

He swigged down the tea and set down the cup, too delicate for his big hands. But it was perfect for hers, he thought. He could see her cradling the fine porcelain, even after he turned out the light and closed his eyes.

For once it wasn't Bosnia that kept him awake halfway through the night.

THE FIRST RAYS OF DAWN streaked the sky over Boulder Municipal Airport. Gilad had been lying in wait for nearly an hour. As always, he was patient.

And he really was more clever than the bungled attempt on the Pearl Street Mall indicated. He was still burning at that temporary setback.

He disliked failure. Disliked looking like a fool even more.

For that, he would require special payment.

Gilad knew all about Frank Connolly, ex-military pilot. His contacts were fast and thorough. Yes, indeed, he could easily imagine the bastard's worst fears.

As he checked his watch yet again, just as he had been doing every few minutes, an addendum to his plan was already forming. Something that would give him infinite pleasure. A very special way to test his enemy's true mettle…

Thinking about Connolly flying without benefit of either plane or parachute brought a smile to his lips.

But his fanciful musings were cut off at the sound of footfalls along the tarmac. Time to get down to work. He stepped out in clear view of the approaching man, who was stocky, of medium height and with burnished skin tone. His mustache was neat, as were his navy slacks, white short-sleeved shirt and tie. A laminated ID swung from his pocket protector.

''Vasquez?''

''Right. You Connolly?''

Gilad nodded.

''So where's the horse van?''

''Not here yet.''

''Then why did you insist I get here an hour earlier than planned?''

''We have something to take care of.''

''What's that?''

Gilad slipped the cold object from his pocket, saying, ''Let me show you.''

Chapter Three

C.J. yawned her way to Boulder Municipal. She'd barely fallen asleep before dawn. And all too soon, Frank had been pounding at her door.

To look at him, one would think he'd had a full eight hours' sleep. She knew better. She'd heard him roaming around the living room for at least an hour after she'd locked herself in. What had been bothering him? she wondered. Something serious—at least the nightmare had made it seem that way. He hid his exhaustion well, though. She wondered what else he was hiding and why he thought it was necessary. Not that she should expect true confessions from a stranger. His past was *his* past, just as hers was her own.

"Your chariot awaits," Frank said, breaking into her thoughts. "And the trailer is already here, too."

"What trailer?" But she swept her gaze right past the commercial vehicle and onto the adjoining aircraft, which appeared to have been built in the previous century. "What is that thing?"

"A DC-3."

He brought the car to a stop near the hangar, and she took a better look. The plane's lines were chunky, both propellers and wheels appeared to share a housing, and its tail practically swept the tarmac.

"Can you actually get that thing in the air and keep it there?"

"Plenty of these babies still take up airspace, hauling cargo—and they have been for the better part of six decades."

"That's what bothers me."

She couldn't help the trepidation that filled her. Too many stories of failed parts on old planes. She rubbed her arms and refocused her attention back to the trailer, where a man in dark pants and a white shirt was talking to another dressed more casually in jeans, plaid shirt and billed cap.

A special ramp already in place led from the trailer's back end up to the rear door of the aircraft. Suddenly, from the side of the trailer, brilliant red lettering jumped out at her: *Equine*.

"That's a horse trailer!" she said accusingly.

"Did I forget to tell you? Our cover is that we're hauling the mares to Lonesome Pony."

Doubly concerned now, she thought to protest, but before she could get a word out, Frank opened his door, slid from behind the wheel and reached in back for his gray, broad-brimmed hat. Added to the jeans, boots and multipocketed vest, it made him look more like a real Wild West cowboy than a government agent.

Though an involuntary thrill shot through her—probably due to the old American western movies that had once fascinated her long, long ago—C.J. tried not to be impressed.

He said, "Wait here while I take care of getting these girls loaded."

"Gladly."

Stuffing the hat on his head, Frank aimed straight for the other two men.

That they needed a cover made C.J. shudder. That horses *were* that cover made her shudder more. A decrepit old plane and now horses!

What had she gotten herself into?

Still wondering a few minutes later, she watched Frank stalk back to the vehicle, an expression of displeasure pulling at his mouth. She read his frustration in his jerky movements when he threw open the door and held out a hand.

"We have a problem," he announced as he helped her out.

"Apparently."

"How are you with horses."

"H-horses? How am I what?"

"We don't have a groom. He didn't show. We can wait around for another one, but that'll delay our departure for a couple of hours. And after what happened yesterday, I want to get you away from here and safely to Quinlan ASAP."

"Horses?" she squeaked. "You're asking me to groom horses?" C.J.'s stomach twirled at the thought. "I'm not good with horses."

He shook his head. "No actual grooming involved. You just have to keep them calm. There are only four of them. But I, uh, don't know if they've ever flown before."

"Calm?" *She* wasn't calm. How was she supposed to keep four horses calm? And in such a small space? Suddenly, the belly of the big plane shrank in her mind to the size of a box stall. "How?"

"Talk to 'em. Scratch 'em between the ears."

As if the matter was both simple and settled, he

opened the trunk and hauled out her two cases and his own two bags.

"And if talking and scratching doesn't work?"

"I assume, being a research scientist, you know how to handle a syringe."

"The rudiments, yes."

He slipped the three smaller bags over his shoulders and hefted the larger suitcase upright. "So if one of the girls gets overly excited, you shoot her with a mild tranquilizer."

Then he took off for the stairs at the front of the aircraft, wheeling the larger of her bags behind him.

"What if something goes wrong?" she demanded, following close on his heels. "Something I can't handle? Really, I'm not very good with horses."

She would refuse to go with him, would charter her own bloody plane...if not for the incident on Pearl Street.

"Then you call me and *I'll* handle it."

"You would leave the cockpit?"

"That's why I have a co-pilot. He can take over the controls."

Frank stopped suddenly and she nearly ran into him. C.J. gasped and stepped back, muttering, "Sorry."

He gave her a curious look that made her mouth go dry. And a pulse ticked in her throat. She could feel it, even when she stopped breathing for a moment until she shook herself back to reality and the fact that nothing personal was happening here. Frank Connolly was merely doing his job, for heaven's sake, which at the moment happened to be *her*.

Then he said, "Try not to think worst-case scenario. Everything's going to be fine and you'll be at the research institute before you know it."

"From your lips to God's ear," she murmured, thinking again of the horses.

Once inside the belly of the plane, Frank lashed down their luggage. "Take a seat while I help bring in the mares."

But C.J. was too jittery to just sit and wait. She tried to focus on the now, on her surroundings.

The plane appeared solidly built, so why wouldn't this sense of trepidation leave her alone? It had to be the thought of being confined with several horses that made her feel so…so…unsettled.

And yet the jitters went beyond the fear of the known.

The unknown held far more power—a villain with no description.

Would he come after her in Montana?

Would she ever be safe?

There were four passenger seats, three in one row, then one extra from which she could easily see openings in two of the four stalls. She came closer for a better look. The double-double configuration—two stalls in the front, two in the back—was open on top. The U-shape would allow two of the horses to hang out their heads toward her.

The stalls sat on anchored pallets in the center of the cargo area, leaving aisles for humans to walk along each side. She wandered toward the rear of the aircraft. Feed and other supplies had already been brought in and secured. As had western tack—she noted saddles and other leathers. She moved up the other aisle toward the cockpit.

The *clop-clop* of hooves against metal drew her to a window. Frank was leading a big bay mare up the ramp—C.J. could see her tossing head and rolling eyes over the raised side. Though the driver led a small palomino that seemed perfectly calm, she felt her pulse surge and she pulled back. She had to get over her irrational fear—only a few hours and she would be free of them.

C.J. glanced down the side aisle as Frank stepped in. He held the mare's head low to squeeze her through the opening, then walked her straight through the back stall to the one in front, where he began securing her with cargo straps.

He did all with such ease that she suspected he must have a lot of experience with horses. She had to remember that, as well as his promise to handle any difficulty.

"Spice Girl," Frank said, as he hooked two tie-downs from the leather collar encircling her neck to holes beneath the U of the stall front.

"Pardon me?"

"Her name." He indicated the adjoining stall where the driver was securing the palomino. "And that one's Double Platinum."

As if knowing their names would make this any easier on her, C.J. thought as Frank dug into one of the myriad pockets on his vest and pulled out a zipped plastic bag that appeared to be filled with apple chunks. He shook out a few pieces and offered it to the mares.

Then he handed her the rest. "Here," he said before retreating to the exit.

C.J. held the bag of apple bits by two fingers. "What am I supposed to do with these?"

"Make friends."

That would mean getting close....

Perhaps later if she really needed something to soothe the beasts, she thought, looking for a place to stuff the bag. The pockets of her jacket were too small, but she was wearing a pair of loose tan trousers with extra-deep pockets. One was already half filled with a handful of individually wrapped chocolate bits, so she shoved the bag of horse treats into the other.

"You must be the passenger, C. J. Birch."

C.J. whipped around to face the neatly dressed man she'd seen from the car when they arrived. He held a clipboard in one hand and held out the other. She looked up to see his mouth curve into a friendly grin beneath a thick black mustache.

"John Vasquez, first officer on this flight."

Glancing at his picture ID and shaking his hand, she noticed his face was deeply tanned. "Mr. Vasquez."

"We'll be taking off shortly, as soon as those other two horses are loaded."

His accent was slight, making her think that while he'd been born in Mexico or elsewhere, he'd probably been in this country for many years.

"Good. I'm anxious to be in the air."

And away from a place that had proved unsafe, even as she'd feared, if not in the manner she had expected. True, the Quinlan Research Institute was bound to be far more remote than the National Center for Aquatic Research, but that was probably good. Less likely that the villain could find her again. She could take comfort in that.

And at least her well-being would be guarded by Frank Connolly and the other Montana Confidential men.

"If you've never been in one of these old planes, be prepared for the noise, especially since we're hauling cargo. No sound-proofing."

"I don't mind a little noise."

"Good. Now, if you'll excuse me, miss, I have some checks to make."

"Go ahead, please," she said even as she heard hooves clacking against the metal ramp.

She only hoped her work on the antidote to D-5 went well and fast. Then she would go home, C.J. thought. England. She wouldn't be afraid there.

Frank and the van driver went through the same routine with the other two horses, a dainty chestnut named Born to Be Wild and High Note, another bay. And then they set up hay nets in front of each of the four horses.

Not that the animals were relaxed enough to eat, she noted.

"They'll chow down when we're in flight," Frank assured her. "You'll have to water them at least once."

He indicated the large resin water container and two metal buckets lashed to the side of the cargo bay.

"Uh-huh."

She could handle that, C.J. told herself, even as her pulse tripped a beat.

"And the tranquilizers are in that pack," he said, pointing out a fastened-down canvas bag with lots of outer pockets. "Top zipper."

"I'm praying for a smooth, uneventful flight," C.J. said. She hoped to heaven she wouldn't need to go into the bag for anything.

"I'll take care of the ramp and stairs," the driver said as he left with a wave.

Frank secured the door behind him. And as if they knew what was going on, the mares grew restless. One snorted, another whinnied, and all four tested their constraints.

"Talk to them," Frank said as he made his way to the cockpit. "I'll let you know when to buckle up."

"Talk to them," she echoed softly, moving so the mares could better see her, yet keeping a safe distance. "Take it easy now, ladies."

She spoke to them in a soothing tone even as she heard Frank and his copilot begin a preflight checklist. Not that she knew locks and chocks from gear and flap selectors. She tuned out the men and concentrated on her charges. As little as she might like a job, she had always taken any responsibility given her seriously.

"These restraints are for your safety and are only temporary," she assured the mares, thinking she sounded somewhat like a flight attendant. Which, in a way, she was. "Soon you'll be frolicking in a big pasture."

The actual words she chose might be lame, but to C.J.'s relief, the mares seemed to respond to the calming sound of her voice.

Suddenly the engines roared to life, as did the mare called Double Platinum. She stomped and snorted and tried throwing up her head. Dismayed at the animal's frustration, C.J. stepped just close enough to give the velvety surface of her nose a gentle pet.

Her own stomach tumbled as she murmured, "There, there, now."

The palomino calmed, but the chestnut in one of the rear stalls seemed equally upset. Her sense of unease growing, C.J. quickly moved around to reassure her, as well. Unfortunately, a pat on the nose didn't do a thing. The mare's eyes rolled wildly and the muscles in her neck bulged. C.J.'s heart accelerated when the animal began thrashing around in the confined space. And when she kicked the sides of the stall, C.J. flew back, fearful for her own safety.

And for the frightened beast's, as well, since she knew how easily a horse could break a leg.

Getting nowhere with rudimentary calming techniques, she thought to call Frank. And yet she hesitated. He would think her a coward. But what were her options?

The awful realization suddenly set in—she'd have to drug this one.

Her hands shook as she unzipped the bag for the supplies. No sooner did she get to the syringe and set it up with the tranquilizer than she heard Frank's voice over the intercom, his commanding tone competing with the roar of the engines.

"Time to buckle up!"

"In a minute!" she yelled back, fighting herself, trying to get near the mare, who was intent on biting her rather than accept the tranquilizer with dignity.

Or so it seemed to a frustrated C.J.

But she had to do this, she thought as the shaking of her hands spread to the rest of her. *Had to.* She couldn't let Frank down. He was counting on her. She concentrated on that fact. On the man who had come out of nowhere to save her. He'd asked this one thing of her and she *would* do it.

Sweat popped on her brow as she made one attempt after another to get close. Her stomach threatened to empty itself. But it would have to wait, C.J. thought, until after she'd administered the injection. Every time she tried, however, the chestnut moved with her and gave her the evil eye. Then the mare would roll her eyes and bare her teeth. And the restraints were long enough to give her some latitude.

It became a dance of sorts, a matter of the mare

trying to assert her will over the too weak, too humiliatingly cowardly human in charge.

About to rush to the cockpit and beg for Frank's help, C.J. realized that she had no options when the plane began to move along the tarmac.

Too late!

She had to do this!

"Now, just settle down, Miss Wild!"

The mare sassed her back.

A desperate C.J. thrust her free hand under the animal's head and shoved upward until the restraints tightened. The unplanned action took the chestnut by surprise—she didn't fight for a few precious seconds, long enough for C.J. to administer the injection. And by the time the mare knew what she was about, it was all over and C.J. quickly backed out of teeth range.

"There, now you'll feel better."

As would she.

Born to Be Wild snorted. Her long red lashes swept over her eyes and she suddenly appeared a bit befuddled. And vulnerable. C.J. told herself to back away, to get to her seat. She herself was still shaking and unsteady on her feet.

But something deep within her responded to the mare's fear and confusion.

Thrusting her hand in her pocket and fishing out an apple chunk from the bag, she was almost surprised when the mare took it from her palm without trying to nip her. The tranquilizer was already doing its job.

Breathing easier, C.J. fought her way forward, legs wobbly but doing the job, as the plane taxied faster. Still unsettled even though the mares were taken care of and no one was hurt, she threw herself into her seat and buckled up mere seconds before the big metal bird launched itself into the sky.

MORE THAN HALFWAY THROUGH the flight and everything was going according to plan. No panicked pleas for help from C.J., either, Frank thought.

Back in disguise from the moment she'd left her bedroom that morning—a too-large pantsuit and hair twisted and secured away from her face with a big, plain clip—she'd almost convinced him that he'd imagined the attraction he'd felt the night before. Almost. That moment of connection in the plane had brought those feelings tumbling back.

Not that she would show him her soft side after he'd left her to be terrorized by four ferocious mares.

Frank grinned and snorted to himself.

"Something wrong?" his copilot asked.

"Wrong? No." Nothing, now that he had C.J. out of harm's path. "Just thought of something amusing, is all."

"Mmm."

Which was about the extent of Vasquez's conversational skills. He'd barely volunteered a word not related to work since the plane had taken off. Frank ignored a trickle of discomfort—he'd never been paired with such a reticent pilot. At least Vasquez was competent. And he himself was unsettled in general. Maybe he just needed to stretch.

"Think you can handle the controls for a while?"

Vasquez slid him a sideways glance. "Isn't that why I'm here?"

A peculiar way to answer a question—with another question. Just another facet of the man's odd nature, Frank guessed, like the zippered paratrooper boots he

wore. Not that he would bother asking the man about
them.

Before exiting the cockpit, Frank took stock of their
position. They were about fifteen minutes from the
Montana border. He wondered if Daniel had made any
headway in identifying C.J.'s attacker. He'd get the
answer to that one soon enough.

He turned away, his gaze sweeping over his copilot,
whose concentration was on the controls. His head was
bent forward slightly, and Frank noticed a dark stain
along the man's shirt collar.

As if aware of the close scrutiny, Vasquez glanced
up at him in question.

Frank nodded and left the cockpit.

As he entered the cabin area, he didn't know what
to expect—certainly not C.J. curled in her seat, half
turned toward her charges, who stood calmly staring at
him. Spice Girl was munching the last of her hay.

And C.J. was dead asleep.

Her mouth hung open slightly. And he imagined he
could hear the softness of her breath against the harsh
power of the engines. Her hair was half wrested from
its clip, and her glasses yet again sat crookedly on her
delicate nose.

Frank couldn't help himself. He reached over to
straighten the metal frames on her face. And while his
hand was there, he couldn't stop himself from brushing
knuckles over her cheek, smoothing back the loose
hair.

Suddenly her eyes shot open and with a strangled
breath, she sat straight up.

"The horses...what..."

"They're fine."

She checked her watch. "No, they're not. I haven't given them water—"

"I'll do it. You're still half asleep."

She sat there looking a little dazed, while he filled one of the buckets and offered it to Spice Girl, who immediately dipped her nose into the water and began siphoning.

"I am awake now," C.J. said, launching herself out of the seat. "I can do that."

Frank crooked an eyebrow at her. "What? You want me out of here already? Surely you trust my copilot at the controls for a little while."

She shoved her hands behind her back. "It's just that I'm usually on top of things."

The statement was reminiscent of Jewel telling him how responsible she was. The girl had taken the task he'd given her with Silver very seriously also.

Not that he was comparing C.J. to the twelve-year-old. She was every inch a woman. And yet…in some ways, she did seem younger than her years would indicate…and she seemed unsure of herself. Around all men?

Or did *he* make her feel insecure somehow?

C.J. walked around him and moved toward the back of the plane. As he switched the water bucket to the palomino, he realized she was checking on the chestnut without getting too close.

"She's asleep, huh?"

"With some help," C.J. said. "It's a good thing you came prepared with that tranq."

"That's me. A real Boy Scout. You know our motto—*Be Prepared.*"

"For anything?"

"Most things," he muttered.

For Frank realized that he wasn't prepared for *her,* for the shock of being attracted to another woman so soon.

After refilling the bucket, he watered High Note, all the while surreptitiously watching C.J. A scientist of some repute, she seemed unsure of herself in her present situation, unable to look him square in the eye.

Oddly enough, he found her uncertainty charming.

Born to Be Wild woke up long enough to take a short drink, then dozed once more. He turned to find C.J. looking amused.

"I just got it. Born to Be Wild. High Note. Double Platinum. Spice Girl. Music—all their names are connected with music."

"Their owner is a pop singer," Frank said.

"Anyone famous?"

"Ever heard of Jill and Her Four Jacks?"

"Afraid not."

"Then I guess not famous enough."

Her lips quivered into a smile that lit up her face. She really was pretty when she smiled.

"So this Jill still owns the mares?" she asked.

He nodded. "They're ladies of leisure now, retired from the racing circuit to be introduced to some good ole boys to make baby racehorses. Jill wanted Sierra Sunrise to be one of the daddies, and since we own him..."

"Ah, I see."

Her discomfort seemingly renewed—at the turn of the conversation? he wondered—she checked her watch.

"So we're almost there?" she asked.

"We'll be crossing the Wyoming-Montana border

any minute now. In a couple of hours, you'll be settled
into your new digs.''

"You will be staying at the research institute, as
well, won't you?''

"Actually, I've got a cabin on Lonesome Pony,
which is up the road a piece.''

"Oh, I thought—''

"If you're worried about safety, you'll be guarded
at all times.''

"But not by you.''

"Not unless I'm assigned.''

"Which isn't exactly likely, is it?'' she asked. "You
being a pilot and all.''

Though her expression remained neutral, Frank had
the distinct impression that C.J. was disappointed. She
obviously saw him as some kind of knight in shining
armor because of his saving her, when all he'd been
was lucky.

"I'd better get back to the cockpit.''

"Right.''

Pure luck had put him on her trail at the exact time
she was being attacked.

Pure luck that the attacker had given up so easily.

That fact still bothered him as he set down the
bucket and moved forward.

The bastard had gone to considerable trouble to stage
the attack. Why *would* he give up so easily? Unless he
figured he'd have another shot at C.J.

Frank worried over it as he reentered the cockpit.

Vasquez didn't seem to hear him and Frank froze
for a moment as the man worked the controls and the
plane adjusted slightly. Almost imperceptibly.

Changing direction?

Frank frowned. What the hell did Vasquez think he

was doing? He came up behind the man, his gaze once again drawn to the stained collar. The skin there appeared a shade paler than the flesh higher on the man's neck, as if the color had actually rubbed off...and the color was definitely a shade darker than his arms were.

Makeup?

Why the hell would a pilot be wearing makeup?

Only one reason came to mind.

Before Frank could decide how to react, the choice was taken from him.

The man who called himself Vasquez turned in his seat just enough so Frank could see the gun in his hand.

Chapter Four

"Don't be a fool!" Frank said. "You pull that trigger and we're all in trouble."

The plane was pressurized only so long as it was sealed. A bullet hole would require they wear oxygen masks—meaning the horses would die for sure, and maybe them, too. And the slimy bastard knew it, counted on it to keep him in line, Frank thought.

"We'd be in trouble only if I miss you, which would be difficult at this range, so I suggest you don't try any fancy moves."

Playing along for the moment, Frank stayed where he was and glanced out the cockpit windows. Just ahead, mountainous terrain. They were flying low, approaching the Pryor Mountains. Sweat trickled down his spine.

What to do?

Getting the man to talk might buy him some time while he formulated a plan. Though his situation did seem pretty grim, maybe he could warn C.J.

"Who's paying you?" Frank took an educated guess. "The Black Order?"

A Cheshire grin spread under the fake mustache. "Someone who can afford me."

"To do what, exactly?"

"Remove Dr. Birch from temptation's path."

"Temptation being..."

Letting his words hang midsentence, Frank shifted slightly. Not enough to alert the bastard, but enough to brush against the intercom switch.

"The Quinlan Research Institute."

Frank prayed he'd succeeded in turning on the intercom so that C.J. could hear. If only she were clever enough to remember his old Boy Scout motto and search through his rucksack. He had several weapons that she might be able to use in her own self-defense.

"So you're only trying to divert Dr. Birch, not hurt her?" Frank asked.

"Assuming she'll play nice. My client has use for her talents."

"And if she doesn't cooperate?"

The other man shrugged and set the plane on autopilot.

Frank got a sick feeling in his gut.

C.J. wouldn't go along with their plans for her, he was certain. And he couldn't let her die. He couldn't let that happen again.

One dead woman in a lifetime was enough burden for any man's soul.

"AND IF SHE DOESN'T cooperate?"

C.J. stared at the intercom box, praying she was hearing things. Only she knew she wasn't.

"What would I do with a problem?" the copilot mused, his accent sounding a bit different now—and definitely not Hispanic. Middle Eastern, perhaps? Or Eastern European? *"Eliminate it, of course."*

Dear God, he meant *her*. He would kill her if she wouldn't do what they wanted, whoever ''they'' were.

While she might not know the copilot's true identity, she figured he was the man who had attacked her the night before. She castigated herself for not seeing through him, no matter the disguise.

''Turn around,'' she heard him tell Frank.

''So you can shoot me in the back?''

''Not unless you make me.'' A harsh laugh escaped the villain. *''I have other plans for you, my friend. Plans to give you exactly what you deserve. A very special flying lesson...without a parachute.''*

Another laugh, this one vicious.

''Why 'deserve'?''

''Perhaps I'll tell you before you take that fatal step out the door. But in the meantime, these will keep you from interfering with my plans.''

''Handcuffs? I'd rather not.''

C.J. didn't have time to berate herself at being so dense—she had to help Frank. She frantically looked around for something she could use against the villain. She skimmed over the seats, water container, metal buckets...Frank's ''Boy Scout'' pack.

That gave her pause.

She hesitated, knowing that searching all those pockets would take a lot of precious time. But she didn't know what else to do. She tore open a zipper, and her gaze immediately lit on the perfect weapon.

''You have a choice. Either you turn around and place your hands behind your back...or I shoot you.''

''If you insist.''

But the next sounds that issued from the intercom were a series of thumps and groans.

A struggle, C.J. realized, hope growing in her.

And as she surged forward, a handgun came flying out of the cockpit past her. She got to the doorway in time to see Frank being thrown back against the console. Before she could step into the tiny space behind the men, the engines whined and the plane shuddered delicately as it picked up speed faster than normal. She realized that Frank's weight must have jammed the throttles all the way forward.

The copilot lunged and encircled Frank's neck with his bare hands. Frank threw a few ineffectual punches—no room for him to maneuver.

Or for her, she feared.

C.J. only prayed that her plan had the possibility of working. Raising the syringe as she stepped forward, she stabbed the needle into the back of the villain's neck and quickly triggered the tranquilizer.

With a strangled oath, he let go of Frank and grabbed for the syringe, turning to her, his face a mask of fury.

C.J. flew back. He wrested the syringe free. She could see it was barely half empty, but the medication was already doing its job.

Slowed down, the villain wavered long enough for Frank to spin him around and deliver a first-class slam to his face. Blood spurted everywhere as the man staggered, then collapsed, hitting his head against a sharp edge as he went down.

"Good thinking," Frank said.

But C.J. was starting to worry. "That tranq was meant to calm a horse, not a man. What if I killed him?"

"Bastard's too mean to die so easily. Now, help me get him out of here!"

Though she wasn't sure if she should believe Frank, C.J. did as he asked.

They fought the confined space and pulled the unconscious man into the cabin, where they threw his inert form across two seats. Who knew how long he would be out?

When she turned to Frank, she noticed the blood on his forehead wasn't from the villain's nose, which was undoubtedly broken, but from a cut over his own eye.

"You're hurt."

"He slammed me with that handgun before I disarmed him," Frank said. "Doesn't matter now. Have to hurry."

He moved back into the cockpit, but even as he reached the control panel, the big plane shuddered violently. A metallic shriek set the fine hairs on C.J.'s neck to attention.

"What's that?" she gasped.

Then the plane careened to one side and they both went flying, Frank landing against her. C.J. caught her breath as his weight flattened her to the side of the aircraft.

"Too late!" he muttered, pushing himself away from her. "She's yawing."

He was favoring his right leg—he must have hurt his knee again—but he grabbed on to a seat back and muscled himself into position. She watched him pull back what surely were the throttles. Even though the plane slowed, it still flew slightly canted and continued to shake.

"What happened?"

"We lost an engine."

Her heart surely stopped. "What?"

"Get back into the cabin and buckle yourself into a seat. We're going down!"

"Down" being mountains, all peaks and canyons as far as she could see.

Her heart hadn't stopped at all, she vaguely realized as it pumped and pumped like mad. Blood rushed through her arteries and veins and roared through her ears.

"Can you do that?" she asked. "Land this monster in the mountains, I mean?"

"Be glad it's not one of those sleek little jets that need a long runway. We have no options. We can't climb with one engine. Now, get back there and buckle up!"

Knowing he was right, C.J. returned to the cabin as Frank ordered. A quick check on their attacker assured her he was out cold. She thought to strap him in somehow, but the plane was shaking so hard that she couldn't figure out how. She didn't really regret leaving him to his own devices—he was, after all, responsible for their predicament.

So she sat and strapped herself in for the ride of her life.

Or was it to be her death?

FRANK WAS PRACTICALLY standing on the rudder to keep the plane on an even keel. Or as even as he could manage. He'd trimmed the rudder to stop the plane from yawing—nose chasing wing tip—and he'd feathered the bad prop to prevent drag.

"Someplace to land, come on," he muttered as sweat rolled straight into his eyes, blinding him.

He blinked and dashed the back of a hand across his face. But when he looked again, he wasn't at all reassured.

They were directly over the Pryors now. The images

telescoped at him and he shook his head to clear it. If only he could find a level piece of ground between the peaks and ridges. He didn't need a long landing strip, not with this baby.

A rivulet of sweat trickled down his spine as his mind played tricks on him and he saw another mountain...another forced landing made without his plane...parachute billowing around him, trapping him....

A string of curses dashed away the memory as a long, deep canyon yawned open before him in real time.

"Hang on a little while longer, baby," he muttered, praying nothing else broke down from the stress until he could land.

He was having a hard time concentrating—his head was pounding, his vision blurring. He touched his forehead where the bastard had backhanded him with the handgun. His fingers came away bloody. He *was* hurt, perhaps concussed, but he could get past it, could stay conscious for as long as it took.

Had to!

He could do it, land this bird, keep them alive.

All he needed was a break. A clearing.

And then he saw it to his left, beyond a thicket of conifers.

He let down the landing gear and trimmed the rudder again, inched the plane around, lost altitude fast enough so he wouldn't overshoot—he might not have a second chance at it.

His stomach twisted into a giant knot. He prayed that meadow was long enough and even enough.

That the plane was stable enough.

And that he was good enough.

His focus shifted and blurred. Darkness tried to embrace him, but he fought to stay conscious.

Suddenly he was over the trees. He dropped altitude, using the treetops to slow his final run. They batted the bottom of the plane, tree trunks crunching and snapping beneath its force. Behind him, the banshee scream of a terrified horse made his skin crawl. But it was working. He could feel the conifer sleigh ride slowing the crippled aircraft.

Through the cockpit windows, the ground suddenly rushed up at him. A meadow of wild grasses and flowers. The area looked long enough.

Almost.

An optical illusion ahead?

He was certain of it. Maybe.

A drop?

Yes, he'd seen a ridge and a drop.

He thought.

Unwilling to take a chance, he stayed with the trees, kept a line of them to his right—the side with the still-working engine—and as he touched down, forced the wing tip into the stand of junipers. The conifers thumped against the wing, cracking and breaking and helping slow the aircraft faster than the brakes alone could.

But not without irreparable damage to the aircraft.

The plane shuddered and protested as if it would tear apart. And then the wing began to separate from the body. A metallic shriek filled Frank's ears. The plane's death knell echoed through his head and receded into something far, far away, even as the canyon vista before him telescoped back.

This time he couldn't prevent it...

The warped aircraft came to a shuddering stop mere yards from a deadly drop.

...and the darkness finally claimed him.

C.J. OPENED HER EYES and with amazement realized that she was still alive and more shaken than hurt. She tested her limbs. All functional. But a tender spot on the back of her head convinced her that she must have been knocked out. Probably flying debris. Her head throbbed a bit. She unbuckled her belt and carefully rose from her seat.

The horses whinnied pitifully, and the palomino threw up her head and stomped in protest. She had to check on them, make sure they were all right. The thought of one of them breaking a leg twisted her stomach into a knot.

Wondering how long she'd been out, she tested herself. Her legs shook, but they held...until she realized their attacker had vanished.

Then her knees threatened to buckle under her.

She'd feared the tranquilizer had been enough to kill him, and now he was gone.

Where was he?

Fearing for Frank, dreading the thought of the supposed Vasquez having the agent at his mercy, she fought the slant of the plane, which lay beached to one side as if part of the landing gear had given way.

"Wrong way, Dr. Birch."

C.J. whipped around to find the knave sliding from the far aisle along the horse stalls. He seemed vital enough—not to mention threatening. A half vial of tranquilizer had hardly slowed him down.

She backed up. "Do not come near me!"

He stopped. "No need to be afraid. I'm here to make

you a more lucrative deal than the one you have with the Quinlan Research Institute. The Black Order will pay you very well for your services.''

''Money isn't everything, though I doubt someone like you would agree,'' she said stiffly. ''I need to take pride in my work.''

She didn't say there would be no pride working for scum.

''As do I,'' he agreed. ''So we have a basis for negotiation, then.''

''Like bloody hell!''

''Suit yourself.'' His voice was calm but determined. ''We can do this the easy way or the hard way, but *either* way, you're coming with me.''

The threat prompted her to look around wildly for some form of protection. Then she remembered the handgun. Where had it landed?

Aware that he was moving toward her again, she said, ''Stay back!''

But this time he kept coming. She ducked low and spotted the weapon under one of the seats.

''You can't hide from me, Dr. Birch,'' he said as she crouched even lower.

What had happened to Frank? she wondered, hearing nothing from the cockpit. Had the villain already slain him?

Pulse thrumming with fear and fury, C.J. reached for the gun. ''I'm warning you—''

''Warning?''

Harsh laughter, too close, scraped along C.J.'s spine. She got her fingers on the metal and edged it to her.

''You don't have a syringe in your hand now.''

C.J. whipped the handgun out from under the seat and shifted onto her back so he could see it. ''No syringe, but I assume this will do.'' Her hands were surprisingly steady as she aimed at his heart.

''You're not going to use that on me.''

He was looming over her, so close she could see the whites of his eyes.

''Do you really want to take that chance? I learned to shoot when I was fourteen. I was a crack shot by fifteen. I shan't hesitate to put one bullet in your dark heart and another between your eyes. But only if you force my hand.'' He couldn't be certain that she was bluffing. ''Go ahead, test me, come closer. I can hardly miss you from this distance.''

A shadow of doubt crossed his rough features and he glared at her, his dark eyes narrowing. ''You win this round, Dr. Birch. Just know that unless you change your mind about working for the Black Order, you'll never be safe.'' He started backing away. ''Never. And you'll have to come out of this plane some time.'' He lowered his voice to a menacing growl. ''Keep in mind that I'll be waiting for you out there.''

C.J. thought to tell him that he wasn't going anywhere, but how was she supposed to back that up? She could shoot him, certainly, but that was the only way she could stop him. And she had never before shot an animal, much less a human being.

Besides, if she were busy covering him, who would see to Frank Connolly?

So she let the fake Vasquez move away from her, though she never took her eyes from him. By the time she returned to her feet, he'd already opened the cargo door. Thinking he would just slip out, she was startled when he disappeared in the other direction for a moment, then reappeared with one of the horses—the one called High Note—already bridled and saddled.

"What do you think you're about?"

"You don't imagine I'm going to walk out of these mountains when I can ride, do you?"

"Leave her be or I *will* shoot you."

"You'll kill me over a horse? I don't think you have that in you," he said, sounding every bit as if he had it in him. "But in any case, you'll have to catch me first."

Laughing, he launched himself out the cargo door, the end of the leather reins in hand. High Note tried to back away from the opening, but he jerked the reins and yelled something in a language that C.J. didn't recognize. Next thing she knew, the mare bolted forward and was gone.

C.J. ran to the opening just as the villain swung himself into the saddle.

"Be seeing you soon!" he promised.

Then with a mocking salute, he rode off.

Not trusting that he wouldn't come back for a sneak attack, C.J. fought with the heavy cargo door. Luckily it had gone undamaged. She was able to close and lock it without too much fuss.

A quick visual inspection of the other mares told her they seemed unharmed, if nervous. They could wait.

She didn't know if Frank could.

She didn't know if he was alive.

Finally, she could find out. Something terrible must have happened to him or he would have come to *her* aid. That thought was uppermost in her mind all the way to the cockpit, where she found him crumpled on the floor, unconscious.

"Frank, be all right, please," she murmured as she

fought the tiny space to get to him. "You must be all right."

Holding her breath and praying that he was alive, she dropped to her knees and pulled him into her arms.

Chapter Five

"Frank, please wake up, please. Listen to me. Concentrate. Follow the sound of my voice. I need you, Frank. The horses need you. Wake up for us."

Frank spun through a cocoon of warmth to surface in C.J.'s arms. With his head sheltered against the softness of her breasts, he had no incentive to rouse himself.

Truth be told, he was roused enough as it was....

He watched her face for a moment through lowered lids and the thickness of his lashes. She appeared concerned...more...on the verge of breaking...and he knew he couldn't let her worry about him a moment longer.

A mental push and a moan escaped him. Against a haze of pain, he opened his eyes fully and blinked her into focus.

"We made it," he said.

"Thank goodness—you had me so worried." C.J.'s expression cleared and that special smile of hers lit her from the inside out. "But you're all right, after all!"

"Among the living, anyway." In no hurry to leave her arms, he didn't attempt it. Just another minute, then he would get up. "How long have I been down for the count?"

"I'm not exactly sure. Maybe fifteen or twenty minutes. I was out myself for a while."

And then he remembered....

"What about the fake Vasquez?"

"Gone," she said.

"How?"

She reached back and fumbled with something. "I used his own weapon against him."

Suddenly the handgun was in his face.

"Careful with that thing."

"Don't worry. I am familiar with firearms."

"You shot him?"

"Of course not. I have never shot any living thing. He took one of the horses and rode off."

"And, after all his trouble, he just left you behind?"

"I gave him no choice. He was lucky that he didn't try my patience more than he did, or I would have made an exception in his case," she said with a bravado that rang hollow.

She wouldn't have shot a man, not even to protect herself. At least Frank didn't think so.

"I was the best shot at Miss Crawford's Academy for Young Ladies."

"What?" he asked, an outrageous image suddenly forming in his head. "The young ladies *all* toted guns?"

"All of us on the pistol team." She removed the handgun from his sight. "I think you're well enough to get up now and call for help."

Even though Frank rose slowly, his head throbbed. And his right knee wasn't doing so swell, either. He stumbled as he got to his feet.

"Wait." C.J. placed a palm square in the center of his chest, stopping him from moving off. "Let me have a look at your pupils."

After cupping his chin with her hand, she rose on her toes to look deep into his eyes. Her breasts were once more pressed against him. And gazing back into her eyes through her glasses, Frank felt like the one caught in the headlights.

"No, no concussion," she murmured, moving away so quickly that he swayed with the release.

No concussion, but there were other things wrong with him. Too rapid a pulse. Difficulty breathing. And other, more personal difficulties. With effort, he broke the spell.

"Let me clean up your forehead, anyway, and have a better look at that contusion."

"Later," he muttered. "Right now, I'll see what I can do to get a rescue party on the road."

But all too soon, those hopes were dashed.

"The imposter must have disabled the radios while I was watering the horses," he said when he found the audio-marker control panel removed.

"What about your cell phone?" she asked.

"If it works in these mountains." He reached into his pocket and pulled out the mangled plastic. "And if only I hadn't landed on it in the fight. Useless," he said in disgust.

"Isn't there some kind of box that sends out a signal?" C.J. asked. "When we don't get to the ranch, they'll be looking for us."

"The ELT—Emergency Locator Transmitter."

Which would go off on its own in the case of a crash. Though he didn't think the rough landing necessarily qualified. If it hadn't gone off on its own, he could trigger it.

But the bastard had taken care of the ELT—he'd snipped the wires that led to the panel.

"Out of luck again," he told C.J. "A rescue party might come looking, but they'll have a hell of a time finding us without any idea of where we went down."

Knowing they had only one option open to them, he left the cockpit and made his way back to the horse stalls. C.J. followed directly behind him.

"What do we do now?" she asked.

"We're on our own."

At least the horses seemed okay, Frank thought with relief. Nervous, but they would get over that.

"O-on our own out there?" C.J. asked in a small voice. "How many miles to civilization?"

"Hard to tell. Could be twenty if we get lucky and go in the right direction and run into someone with a vehicle. Could be a hundred. At least we won't be on foot." Frank ran his hands along the palomino's neck and chest and down her legs. "She's sound."

"You don't plan to ride a horse back to civilization."

"I don't plan on walking."

Quick checks assured him the other two mares were equally sound. And when he finished, he realized that C.J. had grown very quiet. She'd backed off and, with arms crossed over her chest, glared at him.

"What's up?"

"I told you that I'm not very good with horses."

"Uh-huh. Several times, I believe."

Frank released Spice Girl from the tie-downs and tacked her up first.

"Gather up anything we can use," he said. "My

rucksack. The metal pails and water container. Blankets and pillows. Extra warm clothing from your bags. And mine. Stuff them all in one of the smaller bags. Then pile everything over by the door.''

A silent C.J. did as he asked, throwing him baleful looks as she passed him. Whatever her problem, she'd get over it. She had no choice.

But once they got the horses and gear outside the plane, it seemed she *did* think she had a choice.

He was strapping the water container to Born to Be Wild—she still seemed a bit groggy from the tranquilizer—and apologizing for turning her into a pack animal, when C.J. suddenly said, ''I shall walk a hundred miles if I must.''

''Don't be ridiculous.''

''What would be ridiculous would be for me to get on the back of one of those creatures.''

Creatures?

Frank turned and stared at C.J. in amazement. She seemed to have grown a few inches, as if she'd had something rammed up her spine.

''What is it with you and horses?''

''It's a long story. And I'm not—''

''—very good with them,'' Frank finished for her. ''You'll have to tell me later, when we have more time. Now, mount up—if you know how.''

''No!''

She took the ends of Double Platinum's reins and, staying some distance ahead of the mare, began to walk.

''What the hell do you think you're doing?''

She kept walking.

''You're going in the wrong direction.''

She stopped.

"And you're going to slow me down. Get on the horse. C.J."

Her spine lengthened again.

"If you *don't* get on the horse, I'll put you there. I'll tie you on if I have to."

The moment the words slipped past his lips, he wished he could take them back. He wasn't some Neanderthal. He didn't muscle around women and he didn't want to start now. Besides, considering the banging around inside his head and the way his knee was barely supporting him, he doubted that he could carry through with the threat.

Worse, he'd offended C.J.

She didn't make a move.

She stood as still as a statue, refusing to so much as look at him. He could hardly blame her.

Time to change tactics.

"If you don't do as I ask, you're going to get us both killed."

That whipped her around. Her expression was stricken—eyes wide and mouth open.

"I'm serious, C.J. We're lucky to have survived a controlled crash. But the man responsible is out there somewhere, and *he's* on a horse. Are you really so stubborn you're willing to give him the advantage?"

Her face had gone white as chalk. He could tell she was terrified.

And she clenched and unclenched her jaw as she said, "No, I won't give him the advantage."

Frank breathed a sigh of relief. "Then let me give you a leg up."

Wide-eyed, she backed away from him. "I can mount myself, thank you."

Could have fooled him.

And which was she more afraid of? he wondered. The horses? Or him?

A fine tremble in her left hand that grasped both reins and mane was the only visible sign of her fear. That and the chalk-white of her face. She grabbed the back of the saddle with her right hand and slipped her left foot into the stirrup.

Frank realized C.J. knew what she was doing.

She bounced once, failed to get all the way up, teetered and lost her balance against the mare before dropping back to the ground. Double Platinum rolled her eyes at C.J., snorted and stepped to the side so that C.J., one foot still in the stirrup, had to hop on the other to stay with the mare.

Frank waited for a plea for help that didn't come.

"All right, girl, you hold steady and I shall do my best to make this as painless as possible for both of us," she said in a soft voice.

Then she took a big breath and a giant lunge upward. This time her left knee straightened and held long enough for her to toss her right leg over the saddle.

Frank didn't think he could be more surprised.

At least not until C.J. turned to him, her expression a mask of barely concealed surprise. "I thought you wanted out of here fast."

At which, Frank grabbed the lead on the chestnut and the bay's reins, then swung himself up into the saddle.

He gazed around him, through the trees and into the hills, as if he could spot the man who'd left them in this position.

Who the hell was he? Frank wondered, and what did that stuff about deserving death mean?

What did the villain have on him?

A paid mercenary was dangerous enough. But one who had a score to settle was a truly scary bastard.

GILAD WAITED UNTIL Connolly and the Birch woman were mere specks on the horizon before he returned to the plane. A glance around as he walked through the fuselage assured him that they'd taken everything of use.

Almost.

First, he headed straight for the cockpit, where he replaced the audio-marker control panel and tuned to a little-used frequency. Though his contact was waiting, the signal was weak. Amazing that he could get through at all.

"You have...woman?"

"Not yet. There's been a complication."

The frequency crackled and broke up as he sketched a picture of his situation along with his proposed solution.

"...not going...be happy" came the expected reply.

"Tell me something new."

The man who had hired him was never happy. Gilad doubted he ever would be, even when he ultimately got what he wanted.

After plotting coordinates for a rendezvous with his contact, Gilad signed off and returned to the fuselage. He stopped at the pallet of horse feed. He pulled several bags from the top of the pile and retrieved his case from where he'd hidden it before Connolly and the Birch woman had arrived.

Connolly—he should have known the man wouldn't give over without a fight. He'd underestimated the pilot, something he wouldn't do again. It would be his pleasure to take the man apart bit by bit, piece by piece, body part by body part.

And only when Connolly was screaming for mercy would he tell him why.

Then again, perhaps he would never give him the opportunity to hear the truth. As long as Connolly ended up very, very dead, he would be satisfied, Gilad decided.

His thoughts drifted back to the woman.

She'd come to so fast after the forced landing that he'd barely had time to tack up one of the horses before dealing with her. Even thinking about her stirred him.

C. J. Birch had surprised him. The seemingly fragile, backward scientist had more strength than most men he knew. Not physical strength, but the kind that counted.

When she'd pulled his gun on him…

Gilad laughed at the irony.

The incident had prompted an interest in him unlike any he'd had for another woman. His fascination with her grew. Why? he wondered. He'd had many smart, beautiful women.

Perhaps he could put it to old-fashioned respect at her willingness not to play victim.

Or perhaps it was an elusive quality that a man shouldn't try to define.

Whatever the reason for his attraction, Gilad hoped that in the end, he could convince Dr. Cecilia Jane Birch to cooperate. For his sake.

For hers.

Frank Connolly was a dead man, whether or not he knew it.

But killing her would be such a terrible waste.

FRANK COULDN'T GET OVER his surprise at C.J.'s managing to ride the palomino as well as she did. Not that she was doing so in a relaxed manner. She was stiff in the saddle and too intent on staying there to pay *him* any mind. And he swore when the mare sidestepped after being surprised by a rabbit, so that C.J. nearly jumped out of her skin and off the horse. But she seemed to have dealt with it.

The day was warm, not hot, but she had removed her jacket and tied it to the saddle. Sweat arrowed down her back to disappear inside her waistband. He stared for a moment, mesmerized by her derriere cupped by the saddle as it bounced provocatively. If she didn't relax soon, she wouldn't be able to walk when she got off the horse.

Frank tore his gaze from the tempting display and looked around them for signs of trouble. As sure as the sun would set and rise the next morning, the bastard that brought them down was out there somewhere, no doubt watching them, waiting for his chance.

Silently cursing, Frank hoped for another encounter. Rather part of him did. The sensible part knew they would have enough difficulty getting back to civilization hearty and healthy.

They didn't need the kind of trouble the fake Vasquez was sure to bring them.

"WHAT THE HELL could have happened?" Daniel muttered as the men gathered in the basement control center.

"Trouble," Court said.

"Brilliant deduction."

Kyle gave the FBI man a look that set Daniel off.

He slapped down the folder he was carrying and planted both fists on the conference table.

"So help me, if you boys don't chill out, I'm going to skin you alive! This is serious business—a plane, one of my agents and a scientist key in preventing a biological disaster all disappearing. No Mayday. No locator signal. Just…nothing."

The last transmission had come some time before the plane had reached the Wyoming-Montana border. If it ever had, that was. It could have flown off in a completely different direction. It could have crashed.

He didn't want to believe the worst, but he couldn't help the morbid thoughts that plagued him. The plane was old. Something terrible must have gone terribly wrong….

The phone rang.

Daniel snatched up the receiver. "Austin here."

"This is Hal Doyle, from Security at Boulder Municipal Airport."

Trying to be hopeful, Daniel asked, "Hal, what's the good word?"

"I have Deputy Sheriff Chuck Taylor here. He has some information for you."

Daniel's gut squeezed tight.

"One minute." He turned on the speakerphone so his agents could hear. "Now, Deputy, go ahead."

"Mr. Austin, we found John Vasquez."

"What do you mean, *found* him? He was on the plane, right?"

"Someone calling himself Vasquez was. He knifed the real Vasquez and left him for dead in the back of the hangar. Tough man—he's gonna make it, no doubt about that."

"The plane must have been hijacked!" Court said. "That would explain its disappearance."

"That's our theory."

"It must have happened over the mountains somewhere."

Daniel didn't comment. "Is the real Vasquez conscious? Can he talk?"

"He's in surgery now, but he was conscious long enough to give us a description. Six foot, dark hair, dark eyes, broad cheekbones, square chin, diamond earring in the right lobe. That mean anything to you?"

"Not offhand," Daniel said.

Court and Kyle shook their heads likewise.

Daniel asked, "Anyone doing a sketch?"

"Done."

"Fax it to me, would you?"

"I planned on it. All I need is the number."

Daniel provided that and got the deputy's cell phone number, just in case. Then he paced the length of the conference table as he waited for the transmission.

His mind was going a mile a minute. "This could be the same guy."

"You mean the one from last night," Kyle said.

Daniel nodded. "If the sketch is accurate, we should be able to ID him."

"Then what?"

"Then we figure out what he wants, who he's working for."

The whir of the fax machine caught his attention, and a minute later, he had the sketch in hand. He and Court and Kyle all took a good hard look.

"Either of you boys know the bastard?"

Daniel was actually asking Court in hopes that the villain was an FBI most-wanted career criminal.

"Sorry."

"Me, neither," Kyle said.

Daniel faxed the photo on to the Federal Department of Public Safety.

"That really should go to the FBI, as well," Court said.

"I won't argue that."

"The more help the better," Kyle agreed.

Maybe the first time the two had agreed on anything, Daniel realized. Too bad it took a potential disaster to get his men working as a team.

Court faxed the sketch to FBI headquarters.

"Frank would never let that phone out of his hands without a fight," Daniel muttered.

"He might have fought," Kyle said, "but he obviously didn't win or he would be here now."

"Unless…" Daniel picked up the phone.

"What now?"

"I have a bad feeling and I'm not waiting any longer." He'd never been one to sit on his hands. "What if the plane went down somewhere between here and the Wyoming-Montana border? Only one thing to do," he said with conviction. "I'm calling out an air search."

Chapter Six

From the meadow where they'd begun, they had climbed to a forested area and wended their way back down to a ridge with a small field on one side and, on the other, a jagged canyon they needed to cross. Now C.J. understood what Frank had meant when she'd asked how many more miles and he'd said it could be twenty or a hundred, depending on their route. The only thing that could move in a straight line here was a bird.

They'd been riding for the better part of two hours, and in that time, they'd seen plenty of birds, including a golden eagle. They'd also passed bighorn sheep, mule deer and a black bear that had scrambled off through a stand of trees.

What they *hadn't* seen was a single sign of another human being.

They might as well be stranded on the moon, C.J. thought. She might even like that better. At least she'd be able to do some interesting research. In the wilderness, she was out of her depth.

"Time for a break."

Thinking Frank was pitying her, C.J. announced, "I can keep going."

"Well, *I* can't."

She looked over her shoulder as Frank dismounted. His right knee almost gave on him and he clung to the saddle to stay upright. In truth, she feared that once she got off the mare, she wouldn't be able to get back on. But, as usual, Frank Connolly was giving her no choice.

"Whoa." She gently pulled back on the reins. "Now, steady. Don't go taking off on me."

Surprising how quickly the basics came back to her, especially considering it had been half a lifetime since she'd been on a horse. She closed her mind against the memories that threatened her. She'd never wanted to see another horse in her life, much less ride one.

Though she got off with less trouble than getting on had caused, a groan broke through her lips. Every muscle in her body was protesting.

"Got to learn to relax up there or you won't make it," Frank told her.

"And you must do something about that knee of yours or you won't make it, either."

She loosely tied the palomino's reins to a low juniper branch, giving the mare her head and the opportunity to graze a bit.

Taking stock, she admitted the area was beautiful in a startlingly natural way. Even so, C.J. would rather see footage of the place on film or in photos than in person.

That snake with her name was out there somewhere, waiting for her, she was certain.

Rubbing sudden gooseflesh from her arms, she hobbled over to where Frank finished tying up the bay and chestnut. He detached a slender container from the side of his rucksack and held it out to her.

"Water."

She tried to drink slowly, but the dry mountain air had made her more thirsty than she realized.

"Easy."

Guiltily, she stopped and handed it back to him. He took only a few sips. Who knew how long the water would have to last them? Thankfully, they'd taken the tank from the plane, but the horses needed water, as well. And food. He'd tied a sack of horse feed to the chestnut, but she hadn't seen anything more appetizing. And noontime had come and gone with not so much as a mention of lunch.

"You don't have any people food in that magic bag of yours, do you?"

"Some," he said. "When we set up camp and build a fire tonight, you'll have your choice of beef stew, barbecue pork or some kind of chicken dish."

Which meant he didn't expect to be out of the wilderness anytime today.

She tried to put a good face on it.

"My stomach is already cheering up."

Even knowing the food would be reconstituted, C.J. couldn't keep her mouth from watering at the thought of a hot meal.

"As for now," he said, "water will have to do."

"Actually, not." Suddenly realizing that she had a private cache, she put hands in both pockets and came up with the bag of apple slices in one and a handful of chocolates in the other. "Snack?"

Frank grunted as if he were impressed.

They sat on an incline a short distance from the horses and alternated bites of apple and bites of chocolate, making certain that they left plenty for later.

"So where did you learn to ride?" he asked. "Your school for young ladies?"

"I learned as a child." She took another drink from the container, hoping that he would let the subject drop.

"So what put you off horses?"

"An unpleasant incident." Gritting her teeth at her stiffness, she stood and brushed invisible bits of nature from the back of her trousers. "Shall we?"

Frank nodded. "We need to water the horses before we go on, though."

He rose with far more difficulty than she, then grimaced as he rubbed at his bad leg.

She frowned at him. "You wouldn't by any chance have a knee brace in that bag of yours?"

"Didn't consider I'd need one. There is an elastic bandage, though."

"Well, find it and let's see what we can do."

"We? The 'doctor' in 'Dr. Birch' is honorary, right? So were you trained in first aid?"

Humor again. "I'm a scientist. I was trained to have some good sense."

He cocked an eyebrow at her. "Were you trained to see men half naked?"

She blinked at him owlishly. "Pardon me?"

"I'll have to drop my jeans to get at the knee."

He was amusing himself at her expense, C.J. realized.

"I shall cope somehow. Why are you trying to intimidate me?"

He thought about it for a moment, then answered with another question. "Is it working?"

Of course it was, though she wasn't about to admit to any such thing. "Just fetch the elastic wrap!"

Always good at hiding her feelings, C.J. felt vulnerable around Frank, perhaps because he had caught her in a weak moment the night before. But why couldn't she seem to recoup? Not around him.

But, by the time he'd dug through his bag and had dropped his jeans, she had her blush and any other signs of embarrassment under control.

"Sit," she said, indicating a fallen tree and taking the elastic wrap from him.

He sat, his jeans puddling around the tops of his boots. An amusing pose...so why didn't she feel like laughing?

She knelt on a bed of pine needles and, without looking beyond the damaged knee, examined it closely. "It's a bit swollen."

"Bring on the ice."

She lifted her eyebrows high above her glasses without actually lifting her gaze. "Let's see if I can do something about it."

The moment she touched him, he jumped, startling her in turn. She flashed her gaze to his, was caught once more by the havoc played on his handsome face. He'd wiped away most of the blood from his forehead, but dark traces remained. He didn't seem to have any lasting effects from the injury to his head, however, so she'd best concentrate on the one to his lower extremity.

Hesitant to touch him again without knowing, she asked, "Did I hurt you?"

"Not exactly. What is it you're doing?"

Her touch more tentative than on the first try, she resumed the massage. "Alternate therapy."

Which had turned out to be a bad idea, especially since the long tails of his shirt had flipped back, exposing more of him than she cared to see. At least a flash of white caught her attention, which meant that while he might sleep in the nude, he was wearing briefs now.

Thankfully.

"Massage can release fluid buildup," she told him, wondering what would release the sudden discomfort that was filling her with each stroke? "Perhaps we should leave well enough alone, though."

The moment she took her hands away, he said, "No, really, go ahead."

"Uh-huh."

Bad, *bad* idea, but it had been hers, after all.

Steeling herself against unwanted physical reaction, C.J. continued the massage, tracing the swollen area around his knee, using upward strokes to reverse the flow of fluid.

It was only a knee, she told herself.

A human knee without any sexual connotations.

A sexless knee.

But her fingertips didn't seem to agree. The more they touched, the more they tingled. Before she knew it, the sensation spread along her nerve endings to her palms. And from there up her arms.

Soon her whole body was celebrating the very maleness of that knee! Her stomach had grown soft, the place between her thighs damp, her nipples hard.

And when Frank groaned—whether in agony or pleasure, she couldn't be certain—C.J. couldn't stand it any longer. She grabbed for the elastic wrap.

"That should do it!"

Holding one end of the wrap on his shin, she quickly wound it in back of his calf, around his knee, then up over his thigh. Short hairs prickled her fingertips as she adjusted the stretchy material.

Frank sucked in his breath, and C.J. felt a tightening low and deep inside herself.

The moment she secured the end of the wrap, she pulled her hands away from his warm flesh and popped up like a marionette. "There, that should feel better."

Getting to his feet, he muttered, "Feels better than better."

Though C.J. couldn't be certain he meant the injury. Unable to pull herself away from the intensity of Frank's gaze, she felt as if his eyes bored through hers, reaching virgin places deep inside.

Places that she herself had not dared explore.

What was it he wanted of her *now?*

She didn't know how to read him. She didn't know how to read any man. That hadn't been part of her training at Miss Crawford's Academy for Young Ladies. Not that young ladies didn't talk about such things among themselves. They just never had talked openly in front of her.

And unfortunately, she'd never had the opportunity—or the initiative—to learn more about this significant matter on her own.

Lowering her eyes, she watched Frank through her lashes as he brought a hand to her cheek. A butterfly seemed to be caught in her throat—a pulse that fluttered and ebbed and threatened to strangle her.

And when he said, "It's my turn to thank *you*, Dr. Birch," she could barely choke out an acknowledgment.

"Uh-huh."

But it seemed he needed no actual words from her.

Not to slide his fingers back to the spot on her neck that made her shivery and weak down to her toes.

Not to move in so that his chest was nearly touching

her breasts, the very closeness making her feel tight and awkward and like that innocent schoolgirl who had eavesdropped on others' conversations concerning the opposite sex.

Not to dip his head and slant his mouth across hers.

She held her breath and let him kiss her. Savored the movement of his lips over hers. Lovely soft movements that stirred something deep inside her so that she flowered open for him.

Her body…her mind…her lips.

He moaned deeply into her mouth and encircled her body with his free arm. The next thing she knew, she was up against him, chest to breasts, belly to belly, thigh to thigh. He was warm and hard and scarily male.

Suddenly the butterfly in her throat seemed trapped, panicked. Not knowing what to do next. Fearing what might come next.

Flattening her hands on Frank's chest, C.J. pushed him away. Breathing as heavily as she, he had the look of a man dazed by something he didn't quite understand.

Mirroring her own experience.

Unable to hold back a blush this time, not if her life depended on it, she backed away, face flaming, taking small, careful steps so that she wouldn't trip over her own feet.

"I—I'll just start watering the horses while you, uh, pull up your jeans."

At the moment, C.J. didn't know which would be trickier to survive—the wilderness itself, the man who'd threatened her life or Montana Confidential agent Frank Connolly.

THE FLOOR OF THE CANYON loomed some distance ahead. They were snaking along, picking their way between boulders on one side, dangerous drops on the other. A few places had made Frank hold his breath. He could only imagine how thrilled C.J. must be with the challenging route.

"You hanging in there?" he called back.

"If you mean, am I still in the saddle, I am managing somehow."

It had been a tough couple of hours, but C.J. hadn't complained once, though he'd heard a few squeaks of fright that she'd been quick to cover. She'd been unusually quiet, especially the last half hour. He'd taken that to mean she was either too exhausted or too scared to talk.

Frank halted before a twenty-foot drop too steep for his own peace of mind. But a look around assured him there was no other way. It was either negotiate this last bit or turn around and go back up to find another. A choice made simple.

"Let me get all the way down first before you follow."

"You're not serious?"

Frank turned in the saddle. Chalk-white again, C.J. appeared as horrified as she sounded.

"Give me an alternative."

He didn't wait for an answer that didn't come. Holding the chestnut's lead by the end to give her more play, he edged the bay down on an angle. Even by taking a serpentine pattern and leaning back so he was practically lying on the mare's back didn't make the descent easy. And a glance back told him the packhorse was having equal difficulty finding her footing.

Halfway down, the bay braced her long legs but they slid, spewing earth and gravel around them. The entire descent jarred Frank where the sun didn't shine. He wondered how well he'd be walking later. When they hit the bottom, and the chestnut caught up to them with a jerk and a rush, Frank breathed easier.

He circled the mares so they were facing the incline and yelled up to C.J. "Your turn!"

She sat there, stiff in her saddle, staring down at him as if he was an idiot.

And maybe he was.

Only an idiot would have kissed the starchy scientist. What had he been thinking? This was no romantic tryst but a serious situation. Not that romance was his specialty, anyway. Every man had some deficiencies, and that happened to be one of his.

Undoubtedly the reason C.J. had pushed him away so abruptly, he thought ruefully. And maybe the *real* reason she'd been so quiet.

Realizing she hadn't budged from her spot on the rise, he called, "What are you waiting for?"

"For hell to freeze over!" she yelled back in a very unladylike manner.

"Consider it frozen! Don't make me come up there to get you, C.J., or so help me—"

"What? What is it you'll do to me?"

Hearing the edge of panic in her voice, Frank thought quickly about how he could diffuse it.

"Or I'll kiss you again," he threatened in a low and—hopefully—menacingly sensual tone. "Only I won't stop there. I'll touch you in places you didn't even know you had. Before I'm through, you'll be begging me to make love to you."

"What? Why, you…you…"

"Idiot?" he supplied helpfully.

"Yes, idiot! Just try to kiss me again, and I'll...I'll..."

"Smack me?" He could see her outrage replacing fear. Good. "I'll make you a deal. Get yourself down here and you can smack me just for suggesting it."

For a moment, she froze up again and Frank cursed to himself. All he'd managed to do was make things more difficult for himself. And he still had to get her down here.

Then, oh so deliberately, she dismounted and wobbled her bowlegged way to the very edge of the slope, the end of the reins in her left hand. He could see her calculating, but at what he wasn't certain.

For when she began half walking, half sliding down the incline, the palomino picking her way a few feet behind, Frank couldn't have been more surprised.

Or so he thought until the drone of an engine made them both look up. A bright blue single-engine plane flew overhead. Probably some rancher flying from one spread to another. Frank released the horses and waved his arms and yelled at the top of his lungs.

But a moment later, the plane was out of sight and the sound flew away on the wind.

"Damn! We're too far down. Pilot never saw us!" he muttered, staring upward as if he could will the plane to reappear.

"Aah!"

Frank whipped around in time to see C.J. slide the last few feet to the canyon floor on her butt. Double Platinum danced around her, snorting as she pulled the reins free and pranced over to join the other mares. He didn't worry about them getting into trouble—they were at least as tired as he—so he let them be to pick

at the patches of wild grass while he went over to help
C.J. up.

She sat where she'd landed, dazed and in the midst
of a cloud of dust. If their situation weren't so serious,
he might be tempted to laugh. Instead, he peered down
at her with a sober expression and offered her a hand.

Her gaze narrowed behind her dusty lenses, but she
took the hand with her left and let him pull her to her
feet. Then, all in the same smooth movement and before he could guess at her intention, she hauled off and
hit him with her open right hand. Frank's head jerked
at contact.

"I didn't really expect you to take me at my word,"
he muttered, testing his jaw to find it intact. "You're
stronger than you look. Lucky me that you didn't make
that a fist. Do you feel better now?"

"I feel dusty and sore and scared and angry. But no,
I do not feel better."

Her words were backed by the drone of another engine. Rather, the same engine. The same plane flew
overhead, down the canyon a bit.

"He came back!"

Again Frank shouted and waved wildly, C.J. joining
him. Again the plane disappeared.

"A coincidence?" she asked. "Or could they be
searching for us?"

"If they are searching, they'll never spot us down
here without some help. At this distance we're just a
couple of specks between all these rocks."

But he could help them with what he had in his
rucksack. His mind already considering the possibilities, whether or not it would work in nearly full daylight, he quickly moved toward the chestnut, who ig-

nored him in her search for grass. If the plane came around again, at least they'd have a chance.

"Shouldn't they have some kind of advanced instrumentation onboard that can help find us?" C.J. asked from right behind him.

"FLIR—Forward-Looking Infrared. Thermal imagery in television format that can be used day or night for detection and identification of tactical targets."

He got the rucksack's main zipper undone and plunged his hand into the main compartment as the plane came around once more, this time from the opposite side.

"Tactical targets," C.J. echoed. "We are, aren't we? I mean if the FLIR were in the wrong hands…"

As in the hands of the Black Order? The thought made Frank pause just long enough to blow their chances if it was a plane meant to rescue them.

By the time he pulled out the flare gun, the plane had disappeared again.

Chapter Seven

They rode up out of the canyon at twilight, a silent Frank in the lead.

He hadn't felt much like talking since they'd missed connecting with the plane. He'd kept the flare gun handy just in case as they'd ridden along the coulee. The whine of the aircraft's engine had pumped him every time it had swept back and forth over the area, even though it hadn't been within seeing distance.

So frustratingly close.

So far away.

Then there had been that moment when the distant sounds had changed negligibly. Imagination and years of experience as a pilot had led him to believe the plane had landed somewhere up the rimrock and that a scouting party was on its way and about to hail them.

Which had never happened.

Imagination!

Imagination played dirty tricks on a man, especially in the worst of circumstances. He had too many bad memories to think otherwise.

And yet…what if the plane *had* landed, but it hadn't been a rescue mission? Then what?

Only one alternative came to mind.

He projected his gaze hard around the area that was dotted with stands of conifer, as if he could pick out details through the descending dusk. As if he could see exactly what it was that bothered him.

Doomed to disappointment, Frank still couldn't shake that prickle at the back of his neck. The uneasiness in his gut that told him something was off. Maybe the very stillness around them was hacking at his nerves. Wildlife of all kinds permeated the Pryors, yet he saw no furtive movement between the trees, heard no chirped or barked protest at their presence, as if danger lurked and the creatures of the night understood that and waited with baited breath for it to pass.

Absolute silence...

"I need to get off this horse," C.J. suddenly protested, breaking that silence and his concentration. "I need to rest. And so do you. And so do the horses. Enough, Frank, please. Let's make camp."

Turning in the saddle, he saw how distressed C.J. had become. Both of her hands clung to the saddle horn and she was bouncing more than rocking into the leather. She was exhausted and barely holding on, and it amazed him that she hadn't spoken up earlier.

Frank knew she was right but he just couldn't manage to stop, not yet. Not in the open, in the middle of a sweep of grassland where he felt too vulnerable.

"Just a bit longer," he conceded. Away from the area that made his neck prickle. "Ahead, across the valley and up over that ridge with the juniper break."

"I hope I can make it that far."

"If you want a hot meal, you'll hang on. We need wood for the fire."

So she hung on.

And Frank tried not to feel guilty for pushing her so hard.

Those trees were specks of dark in the already gray dusk, much farther than the ones behind them. Another fifteen-, maybe twenty-minute ride, he guessed.

Hopefully far enough away to separate him from the uneasiness palpitating his back.

BONE WEARY, HER STOMACH hollow, too numb to be nervous when Double Platinum suddenly sidestepped around some prickly brush that spooked her, C.J. wondered if Frank ever meant to stop for the night. Since missing the plane, he seemed doubly determined, as if he thought he could get them out of the wilderness all in one ride.

He'd promised her a campfire.

And food.

When they arrived at the intended campsite nearly a half hour later, she somehow got off her mount without falling. She clung to the saddle while she regained her land legs.

She hated this. Hated it! Of all the things in the world that could have gone wrong, that could have happened to her, why this?

How in the world had she gotten stuck in the hated wilderness with no way out?

Sick at heart, she allowed a moment to feel sorry for herself. Normally she wouldn't indulge herself even that long. But these weren't normal circumstances.

Perhaps there would be no normal...not ever again.

Perhaps this was it, destiny correcting its mistake when it didn't take her the first time.

Enough!

Her mind was stronger than her emotions. And she knew she had to remain strong.

"So what do we do first?" she asked.

"Take care of the horses."

C.J. groaned. The horses first, of course. But would she have anything left afterward?

Who would take care of her?

A question she'd never before asked herself. Her parents had raised her to be as self-sufficient as they. Of course they'd gone off and gotten themselves killed in their self-sufficient way. Then she'd learned what it was like to have no one on whom she could depend.

Now was certainly no time to be maudlin. Bad enough she'd had a moment of weakness.

She worked side by side with Frank to relieve their mounts of their tack. Then she watered the bay and palomino while he removed their gear from the chestnut.

"I'm going to leave them all on long leads," he said. "That way they can graze off and on all night."

"What about that sack of food you brought?"

"I'm about to open it. Don't worry, they won't go hungry."

No, only she would. The horses would be well fed and Frank seemed oblivious to any discomfort. But she didn't put words to her thoughts. Instead, she popped a chocolate in her mouth, savoring the taste as it melted far faster than she might like.

At Frank's request, she gathered dry branches and pine needles while he set up camp. The process seemed to take forever, no doubt due to her exhaustion. She felt as if she were moving in slow motion. One twig, one bloody pine needle at a time.

But eventually, she'd gathered enough and Frank

had found a downed tree that he'd split into chunks with a portable hatchet from his rucksack. She was beginning to think that bag was magic, Frank a magician. Whatever they needed, he pulled out of the rucksack. An instant of fancy made her wonder if it was truly bottomless.

Finally a rousing fire was going. One of the metal buckets filled with dried bits and powder and water swung over it. Soon, C.J. caught a whiff of what actually smelled like real food. Her stomach growled.

"I heard that."

"I'm surprised it kept silent this long. How soon before the stew is ready?" she asked, carefully lowering herself to the ground next to him.

"A few more minutes."

She waited in silence, aware of the man who sat mere feet from her, whittling on a piece of wood. Frank Connolly seemed invincible in that he never complained, never seemed ready to stop or to give up or to allow himself a moment of self-doubt. If she had to be stranded in this godforsaken wilderness, then at least he was the one to be with.

Hoping that he would be honest, she asked, "Will we get out of here alive?"

"Piece of cake. I've survived far worse."

As far as she was concerned, there was no worse. She'd been consigned to hell. A very pretty hell at times, but hell nevertheless.

She asked, "What could be worse?"

"Six months in Bosnia."

She waited for him to elaborate, and though he didn't seem to want to talk about it, she wondered if he didn't need to. He'd certainly been cheated in this partnership deal. She never had been good with people. But something made her try.

"You got involved in their war?"

"Military."

"But I thought the United States forces served as peacekeepers."

"You're right. But I was on a Black Ops mission, flying an important political figure into the country for secret negotiations. Not exactly an approved flight. Certain Bosnians disapproved so much they shot us down."

Openmouthed, C.J. stared. An undercover, not officially sanctioned operation. Shot down. Another plane, another crash.

"How did you survive it?"

"Parachuted out. I saw the plane explode...."

As if a controlled crash hadn't been terrifying enough, C.J. thought. No doubt the Bosnian crash was the source of his nightmare.

"I wonder that you ever got into a cockpit again."

"It's like breathing for me," he said. "Take away my ability to fly and you might as well give me a death sentence, because Frank Connolly would be gone."

"I know what I do isn't comparable in the thrill department, but I do understand. Research may not be exciting, but I feel the same way about my work that you do about yours. It's who I am. It always has been."

Without her work, what would she be? Who would she be?

They shared a moment of quiet. And then Frank spoke the magic words.

"Food's ready."

C.J. was more than ready. He handed her the piece

of wood he'd been whittling—a handmade spoon—and set the bucket of stew between them.

"No plates," Frank said. "Sorry, but we'll have to improvise."

"No problem."

At this point, she just wanted to put something warm and nourishing in her stomach as fast as possible. Trying not to remember that the bucket had been used to water the horses—he had boiled a bit of water in them and wiped them clean before making the stew, after all—she swallowed without even tasting the food.

"Eat slow," Frank told her. "It'll last longer and you'll feel fuller."

"Right."

Besides, if she kept on, she would cheat him of his half of the meal. So she chewed every mouthful into tiny bits, then chewed some more. She savored every bite she swallowed as if the meal were gourmet.

Their fingers brushed once when they simultaneously dipped their spoons and C.J. pulled her hand back fast.

"Sorry," Frank said.

"No, go ahead."

The accidental touch unnerved her again. Everything about the wilderness unnerved her, C.J. reminded herself. And Frank was part of it. He seemed at home here. She imagined he'd be able to get by indefinitely if he didn't have to take care of a woman with no outdoor skills and with no desire to learn any.

When they got to the bottom of the bucket, Frank allowed her the last spoonful. As she chewed, she realized he was staring at her intently.

"What? Do I have food someplace I shouldn't?"

She began wiping at the area around her mouth. "Something caught between my teeth?"

"No, you're fine." He tore his gaze away, then reached over and fetched some of the small pieces of wood she'd found. He set the pile before him. "Actually, you're possibly one of the neatest eaters I've ever seen."

C.J. suspected he was teasing her. "What, then?" she demanded. "You were thinking something."

He started whittling a notch in one end of a stick. "I was just wondering what a nice girl like you is doing with all kinds of science degrees?"

"Only three. And it's a long, boring story."

"We have nothing but time."

And she really had no reason to avoid talking about it. "My birth parents died when I was eight years old," she told him without sentiment.

"Car accident?"

"Mushroom accident," she said, her tone even. "They were wilderness buffs, who loved taking trips where we had to live off the land. But that time, they picked the wrong mushrooms for their soup. I hated mushrooms, so I took my soup before the mushrooms were added."

He momentarily stopped what he was doing. "Oh, no—they were poisonous?"

Separating the memory from the darker aspects it invoked, she nodded. "I watched them get sick and lose consciousness. And when I realized they weren't waking up, I took the fastest horse and went for help."

She shuddered at that recollection—eighteen hours of living terror, of being eight years old and lost in a wilderness filled with strange sights and sounds. Of riding a horse that was too much for her. Too unpredictable.

"My mount stepped in a hole and broke its leg and I had no choice but to leave it like that," she said, again unemotionally. Its screams of agony had echoed in her head for weeks. Sometimes they still did. "Eventually, I found a road and people willing to get off it to help. Only there really was no help to be had. Merely weeks of waiting and waiting while their systems slowly, painfully shut down before they died."

"I'm sorry. That's a terrible—"

"—waste," she finished for him. "Yes, well." She stared at his hands, at the way they blindly worked on the wood, as if it were a comfortable old friend. "At the funeral, their friends tried to put a good face on it. Tried to convince me that at least my parents died doing something they loved. As if that made everything all right. The fact is *they died.*"

"And left you."

Frank reached over and touched her arm. She stiffened and pushed the memories—and him—away.

"I got over it."

C.J. fussed with some loose strands of her hair to cover. She didn't want him to think he affected her one way or the other.

Back to his whittling, he didn't seem to notice anything amiss.

His voice rough, he said, "No one ever gets over a loved one's death. We just tend to work around it."

She didn't argue. Let him think what he would. As long as she didn't dwell on the past, she was fine.

"I had no other family, so for several years I lived in an orphanage." Where her intelligence and interests had quickly set her apart from the other children, who had either made fun of her or avoided her altogether. "I concentrated on my studies, especially the sciences. When I was fourteen, I won a competition that brought me to the attention of the Birches—they were both research scientists. A true team, both personally and professionally."

And a model relationship for herself and for some as-yet-unknown mate for some vague time in the future. She needed a husband with whom she could share all facets of her life. Someone more comfortable in his own mind than in some godforsaken wilderness.

One totally unlike Frank Connolly.

A shudder passed through her. Now, what in the world had made her connect the Montana Confidential agent with a mate? True, he might be George Clooney-handsome, but they had nothing in common. Nothing but some racing hormones, a little voice inside her head qualified. She hadn't forgotten that kiss.

Horrified at the direction of her thoughts, C.J. didn't dare look at Frank. So she stared down at the growing pile of whittled sticks at his feet.

Whatever did he mean to do with them?

"So the Birches adopted you?" he asked, bringing her back on topic.

Relieved that he didn't seem to have noticed her lapse of good sense, she nodded. "Considering my advanced age, a very unusual opportunity at that." One for which she would always be grateful. "But they were childless and Jane especially regretted the fact. And in me, they saw someone who could carry on their work."

By the time the Birches had found her, she'd drawn a shell around herself. Protective. Not letting anyone in. And to her relief, they had been perfectly comfortable with the status quo. So she'd felt secure with them.

"Expecting you to carry on their work was a big responsibility to put on a kid."

Frank sounded as if he disapproved. But then he hadn't been in her circumstances, so how could he judge?

"It's not as if it were a requirement of the adoption," she told him. "I just always understood what they wanted of me and, to tell the truth, I was flattered that they believed I was so capable at a young age. I thrived on the work. I loved science. I especially loved working under their tutelage. And the Birches took very good care of me." They had provided her blissful stability, she remembered with gratitude. "I had a good home. Nice clothes. A fine school—"

"Miss Crawford's Academy for Young Ladies."

"Exactly. And Jane and Cecil were not at all adventurous like my birth parents." Perhaps the best part of the arrangement.

"Jane and Cecil? Cecilia Jane," he murmured. "They even changed your Christian name?"

"I was fourteen years old, for heaven's sake, old enough to make that decision on my own. *I* changed my name in their honor. On the day of my adoption, I became a new person, so why not a whole new name?" Her birth parents had named her Laurel—a type of tree—so if she hadn't changed it she would have been Laurel Birch. More reason for her contemporaries to make fun of her. "I had a goal in life. The Birches taught me to make education and research my priorities."

"And you haven't regretted that?"

That he would ask such a thing surprised her. As if

she'd wasted her formative years…or had led a life of juvenile crime.

"Should I? What exactly should I regret?"

"What about missing out on life?"

Noting that he now was assembling the wooden sticks in a box formation, C.J. frowned at Frank. "I don't understand."

"Friends. Relationships. Being laid-back. Having fun. The usual."

"I'm a scientist. I don't have time for fun."

"You're a scientist…so you can't be beautiful," he mused, throwing back her words of the night before at her. "And you don't have time for fun. Is that really you talking? Or your adoptive parents?"

It was as if he wanted to negate the very things she most cherished in her life, C.J. thought angrily.

How dare he?

Defenses up, she asked, "Do you really believe that I don't have my own thoughts? Besides, what does it matter when I am as content as I am?"

"Maybe because you don't know what you're missing."

"As in…?"

Before he could answer, a howl pierced the night. C.J. jerked, her foot knocking over the bucket. More howls joined the first. The breath caught in her throat. Though she stared out into the dark, she saw nothing.

"Wild beasts!" she gasped. "Those are wild beasts out there!"

"Coyotes," Frank clarified. "Sure they're wild. But they're also smaller than you."

Knowing he was making sport of her again, she muttered, "So is a snake."

But she wasn't thinking of the real one with her

name out there…the man across from her would do at the moment.

He asked, "What do you have against snakes?"

"What do you have against me?"

His expression puzzled, he asked, "What makes you think I have something against you?"

"Because nothing I say appears to be agreeable to you. I seem to be wrong at every turn." She raised her voice over the sound of the howls. Her anger was gaining steam. "I do not need to meet criteria for my life as set out by you, Frank Connolly! I do well enough on my own!"

"Whoa!" He held out his hands, palms out, in a gesture of peace. "If I've offended you, I'm sorry. I just thought we were passing time, getting to know each other better."

"There's no need," C.J. said stiffly. "We won't be together long enough to make it necessary." She glared at him. "We won't, will we?"

"I'm counting on *not*," he agreed, not sounding too happy himself.

No more questions. Instead, to her relief, Frank turned his complete attention to his project. From what she could see by firelight, he appeared to be building a miniature log cabin. After pulling cord from a pocket in his vest, he laid a stick over the box and tied its ends to the bottom to keep the structure square.

She couldn't stand not knowing. "All right, what in the world are you manufacturing?"

"A box snare. I'll set it up tonight. If we're lucky," he said in a carefully modulated tone, "we'll have fresh rabbit or bird for breakfast."

C.J. started. She hadn't been ready for that. Horrors of her childhood came back to haunt her.

"You mean to kill some poor, defenseless animal?"

"Nope. I mean to kill one of those wild beasts you're so afraid of."

She ignored the teasing arch of an eyebrow. This was serious.

"You can't."

"Sure I can," Frank said. "I learned to hunt when I was a kid."

"No, I mean I won't let you. I certainly don't intend to eat some poor creature—"

"First they're wild beasts. Now they're poor critters. Make up your mind. And trust me, if you're hungry enough, you'll eat anything I catch."

Now he was sounding irritated. And stubborn. Well, she could be just as stubborn as he.

"No, I won't," she insisted. At his disbelieving look, she added, "Not when there is no need. We're not going to starve to death."

"Are you a vegetarian?" Frank asked. "Is that what this argument is all about? Well, let me enlighten you, C.J. That stew you just ate with such relish might have been reconstituted, but it did have real meat in it."

"I'm not a vegetarian. And that beef was meant to be food. The cow was slaughtered humanely."

"Humanely," he echoed, disgust ripe in his tone. "C.J., are you saying you think I would enjoy an animal's pain?"

His irritation was advancing to anger, C.J. thought, further distressed.

"No. No, not at all." She couldn't imagine him being any such thing. "I'm just saying that I don't want to watch the animal die, if that's all right with you."

"Then don't watch."

Too-familiar words. She wondered if reasoning and logic would work with him.

"Tell me truthfully, how long will it take us to get to someplace civilized?"

"Define *civilized*."

"You know what I mean."

"I told you—"

She cut him off. "I know what you said earlier. But I would like an estimate of a worst-case scenario. You seem very competent to me, so I am certain you can get us out of here in a reasonable amount of time, with or without the assistance of a rescue team. Am I correct?"

"Barring unforeseen circumstances, yes."

Frank stared at her for a moment, firelight casting a hellish gleam to his expression, which was at once frightening and intriguing.

And C.J. was finding it difficult to breathe properly, a peculiarity that only Frank Connolly seemed to inspire in her. It was as if...as if they were bound together somehow beyond their physical circumstances. But that could not be. She didn't even know the man, she reminded herself.

"Could be three or four days," he finally said, breaking the invisible connection. "A week. Maybe only a day or two. I'm not clairvoyant. I can't see what's ahead."

"We can go without food for that long. Actually, longer. As long as we have water, we'll be all right."

"But why should we go without when it's here for the taking?"

"Is that how you think of the vulnerable animals out there? For your personal taking?"

"Now, wait a minute—"

"You have two more meals in your rucksack. We can make do with those."

"But—"

"No buts, Frank, please. I always hated it when I was forced to eat wild creatures my father felt it was necessary to kill." Her throat tightened as more memories resurfaced. "I was a child and powerless to do anything about my views then, but I'm certainly old enough to do what I feel is right now."

With a big sigh, Frank hung his head. "Even though you're sounding like a tree-hugger and not making a lot of sense to me, you win. For now. But when those meals are gone…"

"Then we'll just tighten our belts and go hungry for a bit longer."

"Not necessarily. We can still eat off the land. Plants. Berries."

"My parents thought the same thing," she reminded him. "Now they're dead."

Seemingly defeated at last, Frank didn't argue.

Wisely, C.J. didn't press the issue.

In the distance, the coyote chorus howled its approval that it was safe…for now.

C.J. could only hope that she and Frank would remain safe through the night, as well.

Chapter Eight

Gilad nestled down in a stand of conifers and raised binoculars equipped with night vision.

It took some doing to find them—he was quite a distance away—but the glow of their fire was like a beacon through the night.

It called to him, invited him closer.

But not yet.

He would sleep first while they bemoaned their plight and made plans that would never come to light. Then, when he was well rested and they were dead asleep, he would strike.

The game was getting interesting now. Of course he had cheated. He could simply have followed on horseback, staying far enough in the distance that Connolly wouldn't spot him.

But why take chances?

The plane had done the trick. It had taken three passes to secure their location—too much wildlife in the area, wild mustangs in particular, to narrow down the infrared readings easily. He'd picked up a band of wild horses not far from here—undoubtedly three bachelors since there were no foals. That had thrown him off for a while.

But once he'd realized he was on the wrong lead, he'd continued the search for his prey. Finally ascertaining their position and the direction in which they'd been headed had given him great satisfaction. Only one way out of the canyon and he'd spotted it right off.

So he'd flown ahead of them and, once out of sight and hearing distance, had landed.

Brush now camouflaged the plane that would wing him and Dr. Birch to the compound. Assuming he could convince her to cooperate, of course.

When they'd paraded past him earlier, he, too, had been invisible. At one point, he could have reached out to touch the repressed blond beauty or to slit Connolly's throat, and yet they'd never even known he was there.

They would know soon, however.

Patience was one of his few virtues, but he was running out of it.

He'd waited all this time to deliver up justice, but justice was about to be served, Gilad thought with satisfaction.

The fruit of his labor would be that much sweeter for it when Frank Connolly was finally dead!

DANIEL EXITED the control center alone, mentally conceding temporary defeat. *Temporary* being the key word, he assured himself. Tomorrow would bring a new dawn, a new search. They'd find Frank and Dr. Birch before it was…

He shook away the negative thought and paused for a moment in the upstairs study before going on.

Kyle and Court had preceded him a quarter of an hour ago, and Daniel knew they'd set themselves down to the dinner table. He could hear quiet murmurings coming from the dining area. He didn't have the heart to join them.

But upon trying to get by them all to his personal quarters without anyone noticing, he heard Dale McMurty call him. "Daniel Austin, get yourself in here and have a proper dinner!"

That was the trouble with a living area that was one big open space—no privacy. He crossed to the archway where he could look down the long table heavily laden with aromatic if mostly ignored food. Seemed that everyone was having trouble eating tonight.

"Don't have much of an appetite," he muttered, knowing that he would have to tell them.

Everyone was there except little Molly, whom Kyle must have put to bed early. Their expressions expectant, they all looked to him as their leader. Kyle and Court. Whitney. Patrick and Dale. And above all, Jewel. The girl had taken a shine to Frank, and when she'd heard about the plane being missing, she'd gone all quiet, had moused around the house unlike herself all day.

For the moment, however, her young face was bright and hopeful, and Daniel most regretted disappointing her. But the twelve-year-old was savvy. One good look at his expression and she drew back into herself.

"No news?" Whitney asked, poking at a piece of meat on her plate.

"Not about Frank."

"What, then?" Court asked.

Daniel flashed a significant look in Jewel's direction. He wasn't about to talk in front of her.

Dale caught on right away.

"Jewel, sweetheart, I saved all the trimmings and cores from the apples that we put in those pies we baked this afternoon. I thought you might give them to Silver. I left it all in a plastic bag on the counter. You go get it and give that big old horse a treat.''

Jewel's chair scraped back so fast it almost tilted over. Kyle flashed out a hand and righted it.

''I can't let Frank down,'' Jewel said, her young voice quivering. ''Not when he asked me special to take care of Silver.''

Her eyes swam with unshed tears as she whipped out of the room and into the kitchen.

Patrick shook his head and set down his fork. ''Girl's gonna lose it if anything happens to Frank. She can't take no more losses.''

''She's your blood, Patrick McMurty,'' Dale stated, for once playing it straight with her husband. ''Whatever happens, our granddaughter will be just fine.''

Whitney pushed herself away from the table. ''I expect one of you will tell me everything later, but right now, I think Jewel needs some company.''

As the woman left the room, Daniel took his place at the table. A crisis brought out the best in people, even in a spoiled heiress like Whitney MacNair, he guessed. This was the first unselfish moment she'd shared with any of them since her arrival the day before. He could see straight into the kitchen area and caught a glimpse of Whitney with her arm companionably around Jewel's shoulders as they walked along the food preparation island to the back door.

Would wonders never cease?

Everyone left around the table seemed to be holding their breath until the door slammed.

And then Kyle immediately said, ''So tell us.''

''Got an ID on the man who nearly killed our rent-a-pilot. Name's Gilad.''

Court asked, "First or last?"

"Only. No one knows his true identity. Not even which country might claim him as theirs. Apparently he's got more passports than most people could use in a lifetime. As far as anyone knows, he's worked mostly the Middle East and central Europe for the last dozen years."

"What else do we know about him?" Kyle asked.

"That he's efficient. Has connections. Is clever— and a master of disguises. Cares more about his reputation than the money."

Court whistled. "That makes him a dangerous son of a bitch." As if suddenly realizing Dale was present, he added, "If you'll pardon my French, ma'am."

Dale merely raised her eyebrows and winked.

"Any word on this Gilad's connections?" Kyle asked. "I mean here in Montana. He'd need some local intelligence to pull this thing off."

"If you ask me, you don't have to look no further than Joshua Neely," Patrick stated.

"Hmm, the leader of the Sons and Daughters of Montana," Daniel mused. "An interesting candidate."

The local militia had its own compound and no outsider was allowed beyond its walls. Who knew what information they could glean if they had someone inside?

"The man has a hatred for all things government like none I've ever seen before," Patrick continued heatedly. "He'd be champin' at the bit to get some licks in."

"Neely might be unpleasant and misguided," Dale countered, "but surely he wouldn't agree to something like help set off a biological weapon that would hurt his own people."

"Hard to know what's in that man's mind."

"Looks like we'll have to find out, but right now, we have Gilad to worry about," Daniel said. "Interpol has been trying to trap him for years. But he's a chameleon. Seems he can magically morph into someone else practically right before your eyes. That's how he got his nickname. The Masqued Mercenary. What worries me most is that Gilad is a deadly assassin when the job calls for it. And Frank stands between him and what he wants. Word is, Gilad has never failed a mission yet."

"Let's concentrate on the 'yet,'" Kyle said. "Frank can take care of himself, right?"

"If he wasn't hurt before he figured out what was going on. And if it was just him and Gilad, man to man," Daniel said. "Under the circumstances, Dr. Birch could prove an unfortunate liability."

They needed Dr. Birch, but he needed Frank as well, and Daniel only hoped that both people came out alive, that Frank Connolly hadn't survived Bosnia only to die saving the scientist's hide.

"THE HORSES ARE DRY, well fed and watered," C.J. said, exhaustion echoing through her words as Frank funneled a pole through supporting branches of two trees near their bedding. "Anything else?"

"Help me get this log up and resting against that pole."

The downed tree had been a big one and the stripped trunk was most assuredly heavier than he'd like. He only hoped that together they could manage it.

She gave him a wary expression. "I don't understand. What in the world for?"

"Protection."

Though he didn't say against what, C.J. got into position and lifted when he did.

His knee kicked up under the pressure, but Frank toughed it out because he had to. With C.J.'s best effort added to his, they managed to inch the log upward, a bit at a time. Finally, with one last heave, they set it into place. Its jagged end disappeared into tree branches thick with pine needles. The idea was to make the camouflaged log look like a tree growing on a slight angle.

An optical illusion—one that would work particularly well in the dark.

By that time, they were both breathing hard and C.J. was eyeing him with suspicion.

Before she could ask questions he didn't intend to answer, Frank said, "Bedtime. Get rest while you can."

"That sounds ominous." C.J. inspected their handiwork. "Could tomorrow really be worse than today?"

"We won't know until we get there. Come on, let's finish making up our beds for the night."

Anything to distract her from asking too many questions. He was operating on a need-to-know basis, and she simply didn't need to know what he was up to. The more he told her, the less reliable she would be.

Luckily they'd brought with them the airline blankets and pillows supplied on the DC-3, so they had bedding. In addition, they'd gathered pine needles and had used them to pad the ground near the fire where they would sleep. Rather, where C.J. would sleep, Frank thought.

He still had work to do and would finish it after she drifted off. Besides which, he meant to remain on guard until he got her to safety.

"Well, I for one shall think positively." She flipped the folds from one of the blankets and set it over the pine mattress. "I shall fall asleep visualizing our safe arrival on civilized soil."

"You've got a real obsession about everything being civilized. Another of those things you associate with your being a scientist?"

"Of course not. Being civilized has nothing to do with science. Being civilized has to do with being British," she informed him.

Frank grinned. "So tell me more about your idea of being civilized."

Settling the second blanket a mere foot from the first, she sighed. "Having a proper cup of tea, for one."

"We have tea here." He put another log on the fire and used a stick to stir up the embers. "In my bag."

"Ah, the magic, bottomless rucksack. All I need to do is think of something and you shall produce it."

"I wish. But I can produce the tea. How about it? I'll make you some if it'll help you sleep better."

"I doubt that I need any inducement but to put my head on a pillow to sleep," she admitted. "But I thank you for your kind offer. What I meant by a proper cup of tea has more to do with a state of mind. With the right atmosphere, with beautiful china and silver."

Like the dragon-and-flower set she'd used to serve the tea at her place, Frank remembered. It was the only personal thing he'd seen in her apartment, obviously a symbol for this civilized life she craved.

"And most important," she continued, "with a place that's safe in which to drink the tea."

Safe. Away from the land he loved best, Frank realized. That's where C.J. longed to be—away from here. That's really what she meant by civilized. A place where there were no physical difficulties, no challenges. At least not the kind that could get you killed.

He watched her set the second pair of blankets over the first. She worked efficiently, delicate hands smoothing the material, long fingers turning down the top edges, as if she were making a *real* bed. Though she hated the wilderness, she was adapting more quickly and productively than he would have believed possible.

What a study in contrasts she was proving to be.

And as she prepared herself for bed, Frank realized he wanted to study every facet of her.

As she freed her golden hair from the clip, it shone more than any brightly precious metal and moved with a liquid fluidity that made his fingers yearn to touch. Then she removed her shoes and, after setting them neatly next to her, took off her glasses and set them inside one of the shoes. Her curves drowned as usual in the too-loose clothing as she burrowed down beneath the top blanket.

"What about you?" she asked, yawning, her eyes heavy with the anticipation of sleep. "You haven't moved from the spot. Aren't you planning to bed down, as well?"

A sudden image of her pulling up the edge of her blanket and inviting him to join her intimately shook Frank to the core.

Imagination!

He would, indeed, like to bed down with her.

Under different circumstances.

Frank tried to keep that desire out of his voice. "I have a couple of things I want to take care of before trying to sleep." She didn't need to know how he was feeling, another worry for her. "'Night, C.J."

"Good night."

Yawning again, she wiggled under the covers and, drawing up her knees, settled on her side. Frank yearned to settle behind her and mold his body around hers, spoon fashion. His body betrayed him. He would make love to her in an instant, given the chance.

What was wrong with him? He needed to focus and not on her. Not now. Not with a woman whose idea of life was the direct opposite of his.

He loved the land, always had, even when he'd gone off in the service of his country. That had been out of necessity, so that he could leave the family ranch in his brother's capable hands. That he was good at covert operations had come as a surprise to him.

Afterward, working with Montana Confidential was the best compromise he could have imagined landing as a way of life. He could be a part-time rancher on Lonesome Pony. He could actually make a decent living doing so. And he could look forward to a retirement plan in his future, one that included enough savings to buy a small spread of his own.

Nothing a woman like Cecilia Jane Birch would be interested in knowing about, he was certain, so where she was concerned, he might as well put anything beyond a professional relationship out of mind.

As he finished what he'd started, putting together poles and snare wire, Frank couldn't help but mull over what C.J. had told him earlier about her parents' deaths. And over what she hadn't said, maybe what she wasn't willing to admit even to herself and after all these years.

Ghosts.

He knew all about those. She certainly had her own.

So, as different as they might be otherwise, they had that one thing that bound them.

But while C.J. was in denial—pretending that she was over what had happened to her at such an impressionable age—he, too deeply, too viscerally, felt the burden of guilt follow him wherever he went. He knew that if she allowed herself to be free of the self-image that boxed her emotions neatly in some safe place, C.J. might find herself equally devastated by her loss, even at this late date.

Frank quickly set up the mechanism and, satisfied that it would work, took his place at the fire, barely a foot from where C.J. slept soundly. Her hair had slipped over her face, and her arm was stretched out toward him, as if in invitation.

Too provocative for his comfort—so he turned away.

With effort, Frank closed his mind to any further imaginings and reminded himself of his mission here: to protect Dr. C. J. Birch and get her to the Quinlan Research Institute, no matter the cost to himself. He would never forget that he'd survived while Irina hadn't. Worse, she had died because of him, because he had failed her.

Now another woman's life was in his hands, and he couldn't afford to be lax.

Couldn't afford to let his instincts shut down.

Couldn't afford to sleep.

Using a form of self-hypnosis that had served him well in the past would allow him to rest while the watchful part of his brain remained alert to possible dangers. He'd done this many times before in Bosnia. He was expert at it.

So he settled himself in his own makeshift bed and stared into the fire. He welcomed the drowsiness that came quickly and let the licking, sparking flames invoke in him a sense of absolute peace.

Gradually, he let his eyelids flutter closed, let his mind drift.

Sitting in the pilot's seat...seeing the earth below speed by...climbing above the clouds...

Happiness warmed him and he floated higher until...

He was hit!

A plume of smoke choked him...the jet spun and then exploded....

He flew down, wingless, jagged peaks and valleys coming up to meet him....

He awoke in a hole...narrow walls...the stench of death, of the dying, surrounding him.

A meal was shoved under the door. He shoved it back.

"You have to eat," she'd said.

Irina of the dark flashing eyes...of the beautiful innocent smile...he ate for her.

"My lifeline," he'd told her once. "You're my lifeline to sanity."

Then one day he realized she was his life....

Frank flashed open his eyes, his only defense against the nightmare that obviously meant to invade any attempt he made at rest. His pulse jagged, heart pumped, breath came in sporadic spurts.

Why couldn't he stop reliving what he couldn't change?

He couldn't deal with his past, not with the crash, certainly not with Irina's death, not now.

First he had to make certain that he and C.J. survived.

GILAD AWOKE IN AN expansive mood. Four hours of sleep had refreshed him, made him mentally alert. His sense of purpose renewed, he managed to put a positive spin to his heretofore failure to secure his as-yet-elusive target.

For once, he had a worthy adversary.

That was good, Gilad told himself again. Positive. This was allowing him to flex his mental muscles. To hone his physical skills. Too many years had passed since he'd come up against a true challenge. His victory would be the sweeter for the challenge.

Not long now.

Gilad took a few minutes to go over his plan and prepare himself. Then he was ready.

Dressed in camouflage pants and matching long-sleeved T-shirt, his face masked in swirls of khaki and taupe and olive, he knew he would become one with the dark landscape. A last check of his weapons and he headed out, away from the plane still hidden by brush and branches.

Stealth served him well. As did silence. The conifers provided him with cover for a distance. Drawing closer and closer, he always kept his goal in sight.

The campfire, its inviting glow a beacon, lured him straight toward his prey.

And a good thing, for there was no moon tonight— it remained hidden in the cloud cover.

Good for him.

Hidden by the last stand of trees, he used the infrared binoculars to make one final check. When he was certain he could move out in safety, he crept into the open and kept low to the ground.

All the while, his gaze roamed the flat, broad area as he searched for anything out of the ordinary. But the same darkness that cloaked him so well enveloped the campsite, as well. He could see only the area directly adjoining the fire.

A pile of kindling…a discarded container…the edge of a blanket.

The last being his goal.

But on which side did the woman sleep?

He came from around the back, slowly, silently, so as not to alert them. Her shoes discarded to one side gave her up. Carefully, one weapon at hand, others at the ready in his belt, he snaked forward.

No chances. He was taking no chances. The taste of victory sweetened his tongue.

A yard from the makeshift beds, he hurled the knife with rib-splitting strength. The *thunk* of the hit into Connolly pleased Gilad as he bent to whip the covering off the Birch woman.

But the blanket stuck as if she were holding on to it. Irritated, he tugged harder—in one broad sweep of his arm, ripping it free. As he glimpsed what lay below, something behind and above him shrieked through the stillness and straight up his spine—what looked like an entire tree coming at him!

Gilad bellowed and lunged to the side.

Too late.

One mighty blow felled him.

And all was quiet once more.

Chapter Nine

A crash and agonized bellow hurtled across the field.

"The deadfall worked!" C.J. said excitedly, turning Double Platinum toward the reverberating sound.

A deadfall being the type of hunter's trap they'd set for their pursuer, one usually used on big game, according to Frank.

Riding Spice Girl and leading Born to Be Wild, he pulled right up next to her. His leg brushed hers in the process, making her catch her breath. Even though the touch was innocent, she was susceptible to him physically, even when he didn't know it. She couldn't imagine how she would react if he made an effort.

"You're not going to see anything," he told her. "It's pitch black out there."

As if ordained, the moon chose that very moment to slip from behind the clouds where it had hidden since they'd risen and had prepared to leave under cover of darkness. Although quite a distance away now, the campsite was somewhat illuminated under the silver gleam. Not that she could pick out details. But nothing moved there, she was certain. Nothing but the flicker of the fire.

"I think you got him."

"He may be down, but we can't be sure it's permanent." Frank clucked and moved his two mares out and back on the path. "I think we'd better keep going just in case."

When Frank had finally told her what he had created, he'd added that particular trap was highly illegal. Then again, he *was* the law, she thought.

Before they'd left camp, they'd plumped up the pine needles and added branches to make outlines like bodies under the blankets. Thankfully, she'd had an extra pair of shoes with her to make it seem as if she was really there. Then Frank had attached a snare line to her blanket, so that when the villain pulled it off, one side of the support pole would be jerked free of the trees and the heavy log would then fall.

Clever. And potentially deadly, just as the name indicated.

Privately, C.J. wondered how anyone could survive the trap.

No doubt his neck or his back had been broken.

No need to stir Frank's conscience any more than necessary, though. As he'd said when they'd left camp, the villain had brought whatever came next on himself. She knew the mercenary meant to kill Frank. And if she hadn't been willing to prostitute her work to the Black Order's cause, he would have killed her, as well.

Besides which, he wouldn't have been hurt at all if he hadn't come looking for them.

Sheer self-defense.

"How did you know he was out there?" C.J. asked, turning her mount to follow Frank again. She suppressed a groan as every sore muscle in her body protested.

"He's not a man who gives up easily."

Nor was he. And he'd outmaneuvered the villain. Frank Connolly really was a hero.

Her hero, she thought somewhat giddily.

He had saved her life three times in two days. On the Pearl Street Mall. Landing the crippled plane. And now this. She'd never before met a man like him.

Beset with some unnamed emotion, she kept herself in check so as not to embarrass herself.

After all, she *was* a scientist.

"What are we to do now?" she asked thickly.

Though she'd followed directions when he'd awakened her, she'd done so without question. Her mind had still been addled with sleep. But an adrenaline rush had reawakened it, and now she wanted the details.

"We keep going far enough that he can't get to us on foot," Frank told her, "just in case he recovers too quickly."

Which made C.J. wonder about the stolen mare. "What do you think he did with High Note?"

"Undoubtedly he turned her loose when his contact picked him up and brought him to the plane."

Frank had already explained his theory about the plane—that it had been the villain's. C.J. had been skeptical but had trusted his judgment. He'd let her sleep a few hours, then had roused her, explaining that they had to leave, that he thought the villain was out there somewhere and would attack in the middle of the night. They had walked the horses out to keep them quiet.

Apparently, Frank had been right on the money about everything.

"Aren't you worried about the mare?" C.J. asked. "What if she gets hurt?"

"Doubtful. She's surefooted enough to win races, so

she should be able to pick her way around a mountainside. And she won't starve. There's plenty of good grass.''

''What about water?''

''There's that, too, even though we managed to miss it so far. To tell the truth, I wasn't looking for water yet since we had our own supply. I was concentrating on finding the fastest way out. But as to the mare, a herd of wild mustangs runs this range, so there is plenty of water around. Don't worry, High Note is smart. She'll find her way to it,'' Frank assured her. ''And when we're out of this, the boys and I will come back to round her up.''

A fact that didn't seem to displease him. But while C.J. shuddered at the thought of spending any more time than necessary out in the wild, he seemed to relish the opportunity.

They were so different. Too different.

Yet Frank Connolly had quickly become the center of her universe.

And there was no helping it—C.J. was succumbing to the situation. Normally a woman who functioned independently, she found herself totally dependent on this stranger. And part of her was even liking it.

Liking him.

A possibility laden with torment.

They kept up the same pace for nearly an hour, at which point they crossed a steep ridge. Then the face of a gentler slope spread out before them.

Supposing Frank meant to keep going, C.J. was surprised when, a few minutes later, he called a halt. They were in the middle of a large clearing. Not a tree nearby.

''This should be good enough,'' he said. ''Even if

our friend recovered fairly quickly, he couldn't track us in the dark. And without a fire, there won't be any way he can spot us until daybreak. Besides, we have that ridge between him and us. He won't even be sure of our direction.''

Any reason to dismount sounded good to her.

Slowly, painfully, she eased back out of the saddle.

"What about the tack?" she asked.

"Leave it be."

"The saddles?"

"Loosen the cinches. Though we'll have to strip down Wild," he said of the mare who had been made pack animal. "That way we can get a fast start in the morning."

Which C.J. feared would come too soon for her.

Exhausted, she was glad to be done with the mares so quickly. Glad there was no firewood to gather. Nor any pine needles. Together, they spread out the remaining two blankets and threw down the pillows. The ground was hard. And cold. They were in the mountains, after all.

But she was alive. No complaining about that.

Still, she was having trouble getting warm. She tossed. Turned. Tried to shut out the coyote chorus that had seemed to follow them. Curled into a tight little ball.

"Are you okay?" Frank asked.

"C-cold."

"You brought warmer clothes, didn't you?"

"Too cold to get them."

"Then this should help."

Frank edged closer and, before C.J. knew what he was about, put an arm around her waist and scooped her in close to him. Immediately his body heat seeped into hers, vanquishing the chill.

"Better?"

"Mmm-hmm."

She was afraid to speak lest her voice give her away. She was warmer, yes. Maybe a little too warm.

Her body was alive with warmth. Her fingers and toes and nose. Hands and feet. Arms and legs. And everything in between.

Heat seeped through her from the inside out, affecting every inch, every molecule of her awakened woman's body. A disturbing heat that would keep her awake, if in a more pleasurable manner than the cold.

C.J. sighed and gave in to the pleasure, wiggling her body in closer to Frank's.

Was that a groan that escaped him?

Her heart thundered that she had such an effect on him. And she remembered the kiss. And the threat of another kiss. The threat that he would touch her in places she didn't know she had.

A heady, dizzying thought at the moment.

For she became aware of the feel of him against her. And not only the body spooned around her. A hardness the length of which she could only speculate lay snugged neatly between her buttocks.

"Warm enough now?" he murmured, his ragged breath searing the back of her neck.

C.J. merely said, "Most assuredly," when she was burning up from the inside out.

Her pulse throbbed in places no man had ever explored. Caught in the thrall of her own libido, C.J. couldn't help wanting more.

Frank's hand at her breast.

Or lower.

His arm was draped innocently across her middle. How to change that? Perhaps if she adjusted a bit, he would get the hint that his advances would be welcome and he would explore her further on his own.

The night was rife with sexual tension and C.J. wondered if this would be it. If she would finally experience the thing that the girls at Miss Crawford's had whispered about, that her contemporaries had certainly experienced, and that she normally tried not to consider.

Well, she was considering it now. Considering it all. Considering Frank.

About having his hand cupping her breast, his fingers plucking at her nipples.

About that hand flattening against her stomach and oh so slowly sliding down her stomach and beneath the waistband of her trousers.

He would skim her smooth flesh, slide beneath the sensible cotton panties she wore until he found her hot and wet and ready for him.

He would palm her. Explore her. Dive deeply with his fingers until he hit the barrier.

That wouldn't stop him, though.

Surprised, perhaps, he would pull back slightly, but he would stroke her and stroke her and stroke her until she was nearly out of her head with the pleasure of it. She would ride his fingers, and when they brought her over the top, would shudder down to her toes.

And then he would turn her in his arms and lay her beneath him and take her properly.

C.J. was now so hot she felt ready to pop. Unable to stand merely imagining what she could experience, she subtly moved against Frank, waiting for a like response.

But his body didn't move.

She tried again, a little less subtly.

Nor did his hand. It lay there along her waist like a dead thing.

She moved her buttocks overtly.

But his breathing—it had grown regular and deep.

Frank Connolly was asleep.

Bloody hell!

C.J. could hardly believe this. She'd been having such incredible erotic fantasies that she had assumed Frank had felt the same attraction.

And he had fallen asleep in the midst of it all.

More fool she.

Obviously, despite the kiss, she really was no more than a job to Frank Connolly. A task assigned by his chief at Montana Confidential.

Humiliated, C.J. couldn't stand being pressed up against him for another moment. Carefully, so that she wouldn't awaken him and be further abased, she inched away from his body. His arm trapped her though, and so she had to lift the deadweight in order to slip free of his unconscious grasp.

He turned on his back and began snoring.

The chill of the night hitting her hot skin felt wonderful, C.J. told herself. Perhaps it would remove the sting of her foolishness and allow her to sleep.

If she could sleep mere inches from the object of her fantasies whose snoring competed with the coyotes singing to them from every direction.

With a soul-searing sigh, C.J. forced her eyes closed, gritted her teeth and tried.

FRANK AWOKE WITH A START as hoofbeats slashed the soft earth nearby. The horses! Their snorting and nickering sliding down his spine, he flew to a crouch ready to fight the enemy.

But the disturbance came from something other than a human source.

To his amazement, he realized they were surrounded by dozens of horses. Wild mustangs. And the mares were responding with excitement. Good thing they were staked so they couldn't wander off.

Frank sat back down and shook C.J.'s shoulder. "Easy," he whispered. "Don't make a sudden move, but you've got to see this."

She blinked herself awake and, giving him an annoyed look, put on her glasses and sat straight up. "Oh, my."

Small bands dotted the surrounding area—stallions with mares and yearlings and foals—anywhere from five to nine animals each. Below their camp, at the foot of the incline, a water hole drew the horses for a morning drink. Though they were obviously aware of the humans and domesticated horses, they ignored the intruders.

"How beautiful," C.J. breathed, her voice filled with wonder as she turned and turned to take it all in.

She was beautiful, Frank thought, admiring her eyes still heavy with the last vestiges of sleep and the honey-gold hair tousled around her face. He remembered the smell of that hair in his face. He'd fallen asleep with that scent filling him. Not to mention a sense of rightness with her in his arms.

And he *had* fallen into a deep, deep sleep. If he hadn't, she might not have been safe from the desire that had threatened to overwhelm him.

A roan stallion with three mares, two yearlings and three foals blew and slurped the water. Then they rolled and splashed like happy kids. From a different direction, another band ventured closer, but the second stallion made sure to keep some distance from the first, who pranced back and forth to show his rank.

"How fascinating," C.J. murmured, obviously entranced by the display. "I've never seen horses in the wild before."

"We're in the Pryor Mountain National Wild Horse Range. The herd is protected and about two hundred strong."

"Have they always been in this area?"

"Folks disagree about that. Some think they're runaways from nearby ranches, others that they're the remnants of military stock from the last century. But the experts say they've been here before the earliest homesteaders. They carry the markings of Spanish breeds—look for the dorsal stripes down their backs, wither stripes and zebra stripes on their legs. Many are that dun color," he said, pointing, then indicating several others, "but take a look at that grulla, the blue roan, the sabino."

"I see."

Three young stallions approached from the other side. The dun was particularly frisky and dared to edge closer to the large band.

Shaking out his mane, the roan pranced up to the intruding bachelors, and with a show of authority, challenged the dun. With fascination, Frank watched their posturing. Neither horse backed away. They reared and pummeled each other with their front hooves, their blood-curling screams filling the air. But when the roan bit the dun on the neck, the dun quickly backed off and trotted away.

"That's a bachelor band, stallions maybe as young

as two or three,'' Frank explained. ''The dun is testing the roan, who means to keep the outsider away from his harem. The dun would steal the mares if he could.''

''Well, it's only natural, is it not? Most males *want* to have sex.''

Frank started at the frank nature of her comment, not to mention her cranky tone. ''Did you sleep well?''

''Did *you?*'' she returned, eyebrows stretched upward nearly to her hairline.

''Uh, yeah, not that I meant to. At least not so deeply.'' Too deep even for a nightmare to intrude. ''I didn't mean to be so thoroughly off guard.''

''You just couldn't help yourself, is that it? *Nothing* was tempting enough to keep you awake?''

A strange way to phrase it, if accurate, Frank thought. ''Afraid not.''

C.J. snorted and turned back to the horses.

He frowned, then shrugged away the odd feeling she gave him. The ground was hard and she must have been uncomfortable. She just needed a good stretch. Or maybe she wasn't a morning person.

Checking his watch, Frank was amazed to find that it was already ten o'clock. They should have been on their way hours ago, soon after sunup. Obviously they had both needed the sleep. Though reluctant to leave this scene, he stood and stretched.

In total, seven bands—about forty horses, including the season's foals—had taken turns at the water hole. In youthful expectation, a yearling from one band approached a contemporary in another. The youngsters romped together until one of the stallions got ticked and trotted over to play referee and break up the game.

One of the mares whinnied, and Frank realized they'd been watching the wild ones with equal interest.

The chestnut shook out her mane and, with distended nostrils, made an odd sound as if calling to friends.

Then one of the foals—a colt, Frank thought— kicked up his heels and bucked in a circle around the adults.

C.J. laughed at the show of exuberance.

The happy sound trailed down Frank's spine. "Lovely."

"Yes, they are."

But he hadn't meant the horses.

He realized her laughter had stilled and her expression had morphed. She was glaring up at him.

What was her problem?

A squeal turned their attention back toward the horses. The roan was driving his mares, forcing them to wheel and turn for no particular reason. No threat now. But he had taken herding posture—his neck lowered and elongated, head weaving with ears pinned back.

The band instantly responded, the lead mare in front, the other mares following, their foals sticking by their sides. They raced up and over the ridge, the stallion bringing up the rear and nipping at the heels of a yearling.

An impressive display. For all his years growing up on a ranch, Frank had never seen anything quite like it. And neither, he suspected, had C.J. With all her talk about disliking anything connected to the wilderness, she seemed not only interested, but enthralled.

As if realizing he was staring at her, she started. "Time to leave, I imagine?"

"Beyond time."

No argument. She rose, stretched, then picked up their bedding and folded the blankets.

Frank noted that the remaining bands of wild horses scattered in all directions.

"Let's take the mares down to the water hole before we leave."

C.J. didn't respond, merely freed the palomino from where she was staked and did as he suggested.

Best he just leave her alone for a while, Frank figured, until she sorted out her mood. One minute she was enchanting, the next forbidding.

And *he* wasn't in the mood to sort it all out.

He fetched both Spice Girl and Born to Be Wild and followed C.J. to the water's edge where Double Platinum was already slurping.

The bay was still saddled but the chestnut was free of encumbrance, so Frank thought to let her roll in the water if she wanted. He unclipped her lead. When she whinnied and, eyes rolling, backed off, he immediately regretted the impulse.

"What's wrong, girl?"

He murmured soothingly and sneaked a grab at her halter. She threw back her head and snorted.

"Easy, now."

From the corner of his eye, he could see the bay prancing and working herself up to something.

"Frank!"

C.J.'s strangled gasp raised his short hairs.

And then he felt it. The hot breath on the back of his neck. And a fine mist when the horse snorted.

The mares all whinnied and danced as Frank dropped the bay's reins and practically tripped over his own feet as he wheeled around.

"Frank!" C.J. repeated.

The dun had returned, alone. He rolled his eyes and blew hard through quivering nostrils.

Frank's gut tightened and his pulse upped a notch.

For the stallion began posturing, arching his neck and tail and shaking his dark mane.

Boy, was he in big trouble!

The dun stopped and pawed the ground, challenging him to battle.

Chapter Ten

"Frank!" C.J. tried again. "What in the world is going on? Why is he doing that?"

Her frantic words finally registered. Frank kept his attention glued to the dangerous stallion as he said, "We have something he wants."

"What?"

"The mares."

A fact that made Frank break into a cold sweat. The stallion was powerful and in a surly mood as he challenged the human for his harem. Perhaps he'd been intimidated by the roan, would be intimated by another experienced stallion...but by a human he had no reason to fear?

Later, Frank might be able to laugh about it, but at the moment, he was too smart to let down his guard.

The stallion rushed him, then feinted. And Frank knew it was only a matter of moments before the animal made a more direct assault with hooves or teeth—equally dangerous weapons. Should the stallion get close enough to do damage, he could use his knife in his own defense, but he had no desire to hurt the horse. Frank merely wanted to drive him away before someone—undoubtedly, he—got hurt.

So, waving his arms threateningly, he yelled, "Ye-ha!" in hopes of driving him off.

Which didn't do the trick.

Instead of running, the dun laid back his ears and rushed Frank, who reconnoitered and slipped out of his way with the finesse of a bullfighter.

Then, still throwing his arms around wildly, he aggressively advanced on the stallion, who in return rolled his eyes and thrashed backward with sharp hooves. Frank barely leaped back out of their path in time.

The girls were nickering to the stallion in their private language, and Frank could practically feel their excitement at the arrival of a potential mate.

"Get the mares under control," he yelled to C.J.

"What? I—I can't!"

"You *can!*" he argued.

Though he didn't know how she could handle the chestnut without the lead, he expected her to try. He could only hope she wouldn't freak if one of them turned on her in the heat of the moment, and that she would be able to contain them.

Vaguely aware of her moving behind him, he kept his gaze on the dun, who snorted and pranced and flashed his teeth. And then rushed him again, veering to the side when Frank did.

Screaming, the stallion reared.

Only one way to avoid the flashing hooves.

Frank dived into the pond behind him.

With a blood-curdling squeal, the stallion flashed forward, sharp hooves coming down in the water mere inches from Frank's head. Far too close for comfort. Then he feinted and flew after his goal.

The chestnut mare.

While C.J. held the reins of the palomino and the bay, she couldn't get near the third mare. Though she appeared terrified, her hand shaking as she reached for the halter, she was trying. The chestnut edged away from her time and again.

And then it was too late.

Before Frank could react, the stallion got to her, winging C.J.'s shoulder in the process. She flew back against the bay, who sent her rebounding into the palomino. Both mares tried to get away from her to join the chestnut, who was racing, nostrils distended, mane flying, tail straight out, the very epitome of her name— Born to Be Wild. And the stallion followed, nipping at her flank.

Frank rose from the water, muttering an epithet.

And somehow, C.J. held her ground and didn't let the other two mares follow as they clearly wanted. They dragged her forward a few feet, but she clung to the ends of their reins as tenaciously as a bulldog.

Dripping water, he hurried to help her. C.J. was breathing hard and shaking and digging her heels into the earth to the frustration of the mares.

"Are you okay?" he asked, taking the reins from her so she could calm down.

"Yes, of course."

Her hands were trembling and he had to still the instinct that made him want to take them in his and reassure her. Touching her was a no-no. She was far too distracting as it was, but should she end up in his arms...

The reins jerked him back to the mares. He took a moment to soothe them. He pulled them in close, spoke to them in a low tone and ran a hand down their quivering necks. Slowly but surely, they gave over. And

Frank wondered if he would have to do the same for C.J.

"They didn't hurt you, did they?" he asked her.

No longer shaking, she was gawking in the direction the pair had fled. "I am a bit traumatized, perhaps a tad more bruised than before, but it's becoming hard to tell. I'll live." Expression stricken, she faced him. "I let you down, though. I—I really am sorry about the chestnut getting away."

"It couldn't be helped."

"You wouldn't have let it happen."

"I *did* let it happen."

C.J. seemed to accept that he was taking the responsibility from her shoulders. She sagged with relief and followed him back up the hill toward their supplies. Frank squished in his boots and flexed his shoulders as water trickled down his spine. A fine mess he'd gotten himself into.

"And in a way," C.J. was saying, "it was kind of…well…romantic," she said.

He stopped dead, and rivulets cascaded down every inch of him. "Romantic?"

"Such passion on the stallion's part." She gave him yet another of those puzzling looks. "He's one male who knows what he wants. And he got her."

"Yeah, right." Frank laughed ruefully. "That danged romantic stallion just stole our mare."

"Stole?"

"You don't think they're going to have a romantic tryst and then she'll just trot back to us, do you?" He could see that she hadn't considered the implications of what had just gone down. "Born to Be Wild is gone, C.J. She belongs to the dun, at least for the moment."

C.J. sobered. "What can we do?"

"*We?* Nothing. Send the posse after her in addition to High Note, I reckon."

A breeze picked up, and a chill shook him.

Her eyes widened as if she had just noticed his sodden appearance. She blinked. Then snorted in a very unladylike fashion.

Frank's turn to glare. "See something that amuses you?"

C.J. grinned. "Frank Connolly, Montana Confidential agent, bested by a mere horse."

"A wild stallion."

"You must admit, it's an amusing concept."

"Amusing?" he echoed. "He could have killed me!"

But rather than sober her, the seriousness of his situation inspired C.J. to another outburst of mirth. Though she tried to contain herself, she lost the battle and giggled like a schoolgirl.

Making Frank clench his jaw.

He tried to console himself—at least C.J. wasn't cranky anymore.

C.J.'S AMUSEMENT didn't last long, especially not once Frank started to get naked.

"I can't stay in these wet clothes," he'd announced, handing her the mares' reins.

And then he began to strip and a very different mood overtook her.

Hanging on to the two remaining mares, she watched him unbutton his shirt and peel it back to reveal his broad, smooth chest and narrow waist, whose muscles arrowed downward. She'd seen it before, in her apartment, but the lighting had been low. In broad daylight, his body was more impressive than she remembered.

And the water merely punctuated the angles and planes of his torso.

Her mouth went dry and her pulse skittered alarmingly. C.J. fought what felt like a panic attack, not all that different from her reaction to being assaulted at Pearl Street Mall.

"Can't you do that in private?" she snapped.

"Sure. Turn your back."

"I beg your—"

"Do you have another suggestion?"

A quick glance around reminded her that there was no privacy anywhere nearby.

As he unzipped his jeans, a flush heated her cheeks and she muttered, "Fine!" and turned her back.

"While I'm changing, would you see if the mares will take more water, then give them buckets of feed," Frank said. "Without a packhorse, we'll have to leave behind most of what she was carrying."

Anything for a distraction from his state of undress!

C.J. drew the horses back toward the water hole.

Odd, though they had given her a good scare along with the stallion, she was getting used to handling them. The trauma of her childhood might never have happened.

Only it had.

Concerned as always about the welfare of any animal, she asked Frank, "You're planning to abandon their feed?"

"They'll get along on the wild grasses."

The mustangs certainly hadn't suffered, C.J. decided. So she concentrated on watering the mares, who were calmer now that the wild horses had vanished.

How privileged they had been to witness what they

had…truly enthralling if scary. Not that she was ready to admit as much to Frank.

It almost gave trekking through the wilderness some redeeming value. The mustangs had given her a glance into the world of her birth parents. She could almost understand why they'd been so fascinated.

Almost.

One fascinating half hour didn't make up for the rest.

Something inside her beat at invisible walls to be released. A fragile ache that she didn't want to recognize.

"You can turn around now."

C.J. started and realized she'd lost touch with the present for a moment. Taking a big breath, she reconsigned the past to the most inaccessible part of herself as she had for so many years.

She looked back at Frank, who was now fully dressed in dry clothing, but he didn't seem to be paying her any mind. He was spreading his multipocket vest over the ground to dry out. He was dressed in a clean pair of jeans and a shirt a shade darker blue than his eyes. Suddenly, he glanced up and their gazes locked.

The instant heat that flooded her took C.J.'s breath away. She found it somewhere again, though, long enough to say, "I'll get that feed now."

"Good."

While she fed the horses, he sorted through the supplies the chestnut had carried.

And when she'd finished with the feed, Frank said, "Pick out a few pieces of clothing from your bag." He tossed it to her. "Something to keep you warm tonight."

A reminder of what had almost happened between

them the night before. Rather, what had happened in
her imagination, while Frank had fallen asleep.

In the end, she chose a change of underwear, extra
socks, a turtleneck and a pullover sweater and left the
rest without regret. If anything, she was sensible. Then
Frank showed her how to minimize the bulk by placing
the articles flat on her blanket and wrapping the lot into
a bedroll that would be attached to the back of her
saddle with leather ties.

They sorted through everything and ended with two
piles—one to take, one to leave. The "take" pile was
still bigger because of the bulky water container.

"I don't plan on leaving it behind," Frank said,
"since we only have that one small bottle."

So they took some time to attach the large container,
now half empty, behind the saddle on Double Platinum,
carefully securing it so that it wouldn't bounce. Better
her horse than his, since C.J. weighed so much less
than Frank. He, then, took the rucksack, bedrolls with
their clothing and the buckets.

"This'll slow us down some," he told her, "but
we'll make it."

Though *how long* it would take loomed large in her
mind as always.

She wanted to be free of the situation. And, yes, free
of him. At least part of her did. Part of her wanted to
feel normal.

Safe.

They headed straight north up a meadowed slope.
Frank was certain they were moving north because he
pulled out a compass from one of the pockets in his
still-damp vest and checked.

"You seem prepared for any eventuality."

"The Boy Scout in me," he reminded her.

"Is that where you learned how to survive in the wild? Some Boy Scout camp?"

"Actually, I never was a Boy Scout. That was a joke. Never had the time."

"You learned survival skills in the military, then?"

"Only the advanced skills."

From the gruff way he said it, C.J. wasn't sure she wanted clarification.

Then his tone softened when he went on. "My dad was a rancher. We lived off the land. I learned the basics from him. And what he didn't teach me, Joe did. That's my older brother. He and his family run the ranch now."

"What happened to your parents?"

"Retired. Though Dad couldn't sit still all the time. He always lends a hand during the busy seasons on the ranch. Says it'll keep him alive until he's a hundred. But Joe's the one who has to worry about everything now. The weather. Disease. Predators."

He made it sound so uninviting, yet at the same time he sounded wistful. "You miss it, don't you?"

"That I do."

"Then why aren't you there?"

"The ranch wasn't big enough for us both. What I mean to say, is that I wouldn't see it divided. That way, everyone would lose. Not enough acres for two families to make a living. So Lonesome Pony fills a gap." He tapped his heart. "And the rest...well, it's something I'm good at, can make a living at and be proud of. At least most of the time."

There was that dark mood edging through his words.

A deeply buried something that threatened to resurface, that haunted him in his sleep.

C.J. wondered if he would tell her about it if she

asked. Not that she would consider invading his privacy. But she couldn't help wondering what had really happened in Bosnia.

His dark mood was catching. And why not? She'd been attacked, could have died either in an air crash or by a mercenary's hand. She'd been brutalized, especially her tender parts, she thought, as her mount's misstep made her bounce in the saddle.

All her aches and pains served to remind her of how much she hated the wilderness.

"I don't understand your love for all this." Working herself into a mood, C.J. waved her hand at the open spaces around them, the mountain peaks in the distance. "I mean wanting to be part of it. Taking your life in your hands every time you turn around. Give me a city and a laboratory any day."

"Limits. You have too many."

C.J. took exception. "I don't feel in the least limited! As a matter of fact, I was considered one of the brightest students at university. As for my career—"

"That's not what I mean. You impose limits on yourself. It's like not being able to be beautiful or have fun because you're a scientist. You can only get along in the city. You can only be happy with four walls around you."

"And you couldn't?"

"It would suffocate me. I never have cottoned to small spaces for long."

"Nor I to large."

C.J. sighed. What was she doing? He wasn't the enemy. This situation wasn't Frank's fault.

"As much as I hate being out here in the wilds of Montana," she admitted, "my one consolation is that I know I'm in good hands."

"You have more confidence in them than I do."

With that, Frank spurred Spice Girl forward, leaving C.J. to play catch-up and to wonder again about the ghosts of his past.

WHITNEY MACNAIR RECLINED in Daniel Austin's chair, behind Daniel Austin's desk, but rather than doing Daniel Austin's work, she thumbed through a Nordstrom's catalog. Specifically the shoe section.

Everyone was in a dark mood. It had even spread to her, and she didn't even know Frank Connolly.

So as she did whenever faced with stress, Whitney shut down and shopped. At the moment, she was practically drooling over a pair of strappy black sandals sprinkled with crystals. They would go perfectly with the slinky black Gucci number Ross Weston had sent her, a gift for services rendered. Not that strappy sandals had any more business being dispatched to rural Montana than she.

For she had done nothing wrong!

Senator Weston had merely been grateful for her setting up a dinner party for him with well-connected civilians after he and Montana governor Haskel had returned from their goodwill mission to the Middle East.

But, as usual, her family had believed the worst of her. They'd read an inflammatory story about her flirtation with the very married Weston, and about the expensive gift he'd given her—illustrated with a photo of an innocent kiss of gratitude—and once again, they had overreacted faster than a Thoroughbred on the homestretch. They hadn't even asked for her side of the story.

And so, with her brother Gerald running for attorney general back in Massachusetts, for the foreseeable future she'd been banished to rural Montana, where "she couldn't possibly get into any more trouble."

Irritation renewed with her parents and with Senator Ross Weston for putting her in this position in the first place, Whitney picked up the phone, intending to order the shoes, anyway. She needed some kind of diversion and new shoes always made her feel better.

Besides, they really would be perfect with the dress that she had *earned* and therefore was meant to wear!

But before she could dial, Daniel came bursting out of his secret elevator and into the office. Hah! Some secret when everyone knew about it.

"Where are the boys?"

"Working with the horses, I guess."

"Well, I need them. The McMurtys, too."

Whitney's pulse picked up a beat, and tossing down the catalog, she launched herself from behind the desk to follow Daniel into the main living area.

"What is it?" she demanded. "What's happened?"

"Something's happened?" Kyle rose from the floor, a tiny shoe in hand, his barefoot young daughter screwing up her face as if ready to cry again.

"Let's get everyone together so I don't have to repeat myself," Daniel said.

Whitney headed for the kitchen to alert Dale and Jewel, who were preparing dinner.

Five minutes later, they all congregated in the living area. The McMurtys in the middle, Jewel between her grandparents. Kyle in a chair, Molly in his lap. Court straddling the arm of another chair. And Daniel pacing.

Whitney stayed in the background where she belonged. Correction—where she'd consigned herself. As far as she was concerned, she didn't belong anywhere *near* the state of Montana, no less stuck on some back-water ranch.

Daniel said, "They found the plane in the Pryor Mountains about an hour ago."

"Crashed?" Court asked.

"Controlled. Looks like everyone got out all right, including the horses."

"Thank the Lord." Dale McMurty placed a trembling hand to her heart and closed her eyes tight. "My prayers have been answered."

"Frank's okay?" Jewel asked, face shining. "I knew it! Gramps, didn't I tell you?"

"You sure did, honey."

The mood in the room lightened considerably, Whitney noted. Even she felt a bit better.

She was thinking that maybe she didn't need those new shoes, after all, when Court said, "I think we're getting ahead of ourselves. Connolly and Dr. Birch haven't actually been found, have they?"

"Not yet. But search teams are going out at the crack of dawn. From the hoofprints, it looks like there's a loner. And the other three horses are together. The assumption is that Frank and Dr. Birch have three of the horses and that Gilad took off on his own."

Court pressed the issue. "But you told us this Gilad never gives up, never leaves an assignment unfinished. That would mean Connolly and Birch are in big trouble out there, with Gilad after them."

"The deck is even," Daniel insisted. "Frank is a natural in the wilderness."

"How do you know Gilad isn't?"

The voice of doom had spoken and everyone's good mood was tempered with unspoken "what-ifs."

"I don't understand how you all can just sit around

and talk about the situation,'' Whitney heard herself saying. ''Why don't you just get out there and *do* something!''

Suddenly all eyes were on her.

''We're planning on joining the search team at dawn,'' Daniel said. ''But this is the first break we've had and we couldn't get to the Pryors before dark. If you have any suggestions, though, please feel free.''

Whitney choked and backed up mentally.

She wasn't involved. She wasn't involved, she chanted to herself. She shook her head. She wasn't involved and didn't want to be.

''We'll go out at first light,'' Daniel said, still staring at her. ''We'll have trackers. And ATVs.''

All-terrain Vehicles, Whitney knew. She had driven one on her last vacation to Cabo St. Lucas in Baja. The half-day trip out to the lighthouse had been a blast... until her brother Brian had lectured her about the environmental repercussions, that was.

''I'll do the tracking.''

Now everyone was staring at Court, who'd volunteered. Whitney knew the general consensus about suit-and-tie law enforcement.

Accountants with guns.

''And what qualifies you?'' Kyle asked.

''I grew up in these parts. I know the country. And I learned how to track before I was ten.''

''Good!'' Daniel said. ''Good. We need everyone's cooperation to bring our man home.''

Whitney watched the mood of the room swing like a pendulum back in the other direction.

Upward.

''I could try a little tracking myself,'' Patrick said. ''It's been a while, but I haven't forgotten how.''

"The only tracking you remember how to do is with muddy boots across the kitchen floor after I've just cleaned it," Dale countered, making them all grin. "You boys will need plenty of energy to keep you going. After supper, I'll make big lunches to take with you."

"And I'll help," Jewel chimed in.

Everyone had a contribution to make. Everyone but her, Whitney realized.

They all chatted away, excited at the possibilities, excluding her as usual.

No one took her seriously.

Not ever.

The sting of being underappreciated smarting as always, Whitney backed away from the scene and fled back to Daniel's office, where she pulled out her credit card to order those shoes.

Chapter Eleven

A golden eagle wheeled overhead, then plummeted earthbound in a vertical dive. Suddenly a second bird—a female—vaulted skyward from the cliff below. The plunging male spread his wings and shot past his mate, then broke into a series of rolls and loops.

Spellbound—as if against her will—C.J. held her breath as she watched the elaborate mating dance.

And equally spellbound, Frank watched her.

Cecilia Jane Birch wasn't what she seemed to be. Rather, there was more to her than met the eye. And though she was a lovely eyeful, Frank was more interested in what lay beneath. He wondered if she was aware of her own depths. He doubted it. She seemed to have shut herself off from so much. Gave herself too many restrictions to develop herself fully as a human being with a warm heart.

Her giving him a hard time about hunting for food had clued him in, and her reaction to the wild animals—no matter how much the word *wild* seemed to inflame her—was beginning to peel away the protective layers.

Before them, the pair of eagles played tag, floating on air currents and brushing wing tips just as human lovers might brush fingers. Frank swore he could hear the whine of the wind through their feathers.

Odd how he and C.J. had managed to stumble on these feral mating rituals. They reminded him of what he'd once had and what might now be at hand, yet out of reach. So close, yet so far away.

Self-discipline—he'd learned it the hard way.

And considering how much he would like to indulge in a mating ritual of his own with her, keeping his distance from C.J. was one of the most difficult hardships he'd ever faced. He only hoped it wouldn't become an endurance test.

Still traveling north, they had reached a plateau that might as well be the top of the world. Closer to the edge than C.J., Frank led Spice Girl to a spot that remained a safe distance from the drop and yet allowed him to see the panorama that spread out before them. C.J. pulled Double Platinum beside him and gasped audibly.

Far below, the land lay in upheaval, with bright red clinker stones topping gravel bluffs. Frank could see an actual road—a series of steep switchbacks descending into the eroded face of the Pryors.

"Water!" C.J. pointed to a ribbon of blue below. "Water means people."

"But how far away? And we would likely have to cross it to find anyone."

He could see her heart sink in the way her shoulders folded forward and her hands trembled as she grasped the horn of the saddle to keep herself upright.

Fatigue had overtaken her, Frank realized. Fatigue and a growing sense of helplessness, he was sure. Both tormented him, as well, but he had experience in this arena. It was far too early in the game to cry uncle.

Getting his bearings, he said, "This has to be Bighorn Canyon."

Fort Smith must be only a few miles upstream, but it might as well be the moon for the time it would take them to reach the recreation area, he thought. Not that he said so. No reason to worsen her fears.

"So what does that mean to us? C.J. asked.

"I know where we are, for one. At least vaguely. So we're on the right track and not quite as lost as we were this morning," he joked.

Which produced a wan smile.

Though Frank had known C.J. for only a few days, it might have been months. He knew how she would react to any given statement from him concerning their situation. He knew so much about the woman hiding behind the scientist's guise…and yet he knew so much less than he would like to.

The nearly vertical walls rising about a thousand feet from the bottom cast deep shadows over the canyon's floor. The sun had set and they were in the open. Strong winds buffeted them, and Frank was thankful that his vest had dried and now protected him from the chill mountain air.

Not so C.J. She shivered and rubbed her arms and pulled her jacket closer around her. "I would say we will be quite cold up here tonight."

"Not if I find what I hope to."

"A furnished cabin, perhaps? We should be so lucky." C.J.'s voice filled with longing.

"Sorry to disappoint you," Frank said. "But I was thinking of a cave. The limestone hills in this area are filled with them."

"Why a cave?"

"It'll get us out of the wind, for one. And no one

will see us inside. Out of sight, out of mind. I don't want a repeat of last night.''

"How could there be one, when we're alone out here?''

"Don't count on it.''

Her forehead furrowed. "No airplanes have swept the area. And you took care of our attacker.''

"But the Black Order wants you. You don't think they'll give up this easily?''

"They don't know where to find me.''

"But they know where to find *him*. He was in contact with the person who delivered him to the plane. If he was expected and didn't show or radio in, chances are they sent out someone after him. And you.''

"You're saying that someone *else* is after us now?''

"I don't know that for certain, but I would rather err on the side of caution.''

Appearing resigned, she nodded.

And Frank wondered what it would take to get another of those smiles out of her. He would give anything to be able to do so.

"How do we go about finding one of those caves?'' she asked.

He indicated an area to the northwest. "We start by following that road.''

Her expression puzzled, she turned back to him. "I don't see anything.''

"Revise your thinking. I don't mean a road that has been engineered. But look for the worn spots in the grass. Tire tracks.''

"Someone brought a car up here?''

"Most probably an SUV with four-wheel drive. No doubt hikers or cavers or mountain bikers with an itch to explore the *real* wilderness," he explained. "It's worth a try to find out for sure."

C.J. perked up in her saddle. "Wouldn't it be glorious if we ran into someone with a vehicle, who could drive us away from all this bloody wilderness?"

Frank would just settle for the cave, but he would let C.J. have her illusions if they would keep her going.

THE CAVE DIDN'T LOOK like anything C.J. had imagined. She would have missed the opening altogether if not for Frank pointing it out to her.

They'd passed through a stand of ponderosa pine and had come to a more frequented path when he excitedly said, "I think we've hit Bad Pass Trail."

"That sounds ominous."

Frank chuckled. "Probably, at least centuries ago. Prehistoric Indians used it as a path between the plains and valleys of Montana and the Great Basin land in Wyoming. If we kept going north along the pass, we would cross the Crow Reservation."

And all C.J. had cared about was his certainty that he knew where they were.

"When I was a kid," Frank said, "I spent time in this part of Montana on a family vacation."

The thought made her shudder because it reminded her of the disastrous trek on which her parents had taken her. The difference lay in their experience and memories. Frank was obviously nostalgic, while she'd just like to forget.

After they'd found the car park—plenty of tire tracks but no vehicle in sight, to her profound disappointment—Frank had dogged footprints for several kilometers.

And then, in the gloom of dusk, he'd found it.

Quite unimpressive, really. A wall of rimrock rising from where the earth had heaved upward a millennium ago. An opening that appeared to be a simple fissure.

"I'll check it out," Frank said, handing her the reins of both horses.

He'd been gone only a minute when she heard what sounded like the soft flush of beating wings. Many of them. C.J. went on immediate alert, gripping the reins tightly. The insistent sound was followed by small fluttering creatures streaming from the ragged opening.

Bats!

And they were heading straight for her!

C.J. threw up her arm across her face. A bat skimmed her hair and another her arm. She ducked between the mares, who danced and snorted at the disturbance.

"It looks pretty good inside...."

Frank's voice died off and C.J. peeked out at him, horrified that he'd found her cowering on her haunches, arms still protecting her head.

"I take it you don't like bats, either."

"So good of you to recognize the obvious." She glared at him and got to her feet. "And you expect me to spend the night in a bat-infested cave?"

"Let's see. Sharing a cave with bats or being a sitting duck for the Black Order—which is worse?" When she wasn't quick to answer, he asked, "You don't believe in vampires, do you?"

"Of course not." The threat of the Black Order being far scarier than bats, she said, "All right, but I carry the flashlight."

He handed it to her. "You lead the way, then, and I'll bring the horses."

"Inside?"

"Don't worry. There's plenty of room for all of us."

Hesitantly, C.J. moved through the fissure, which indeed proved large enough for the mares to pass through. She shone the beam of the flashlight around, relieved when nothing flew at her. The inside of the chamber was larger than she had imagined. Several passages led farther into the earth. Not that she was planning to do any exploring.

Then something else caught her attention. She swept her light over barely visible paintings on the walls. "Frank, look at this."

Frank moved closer to her. Close enough to make her pulse thrum. But as his arm touched hers, the man seemed oblivious to her heightened awareness of him. Either that, or he was ignoring it. Instead, he was avidly staring at the prehistoric animals and abstract designs decorating the cave walls.

"I'd heard the caves in this area were inhabited by those old Indians I told you about, but I've never seen cave paintings before." Frank moved away, adding, "No wonder the Crow consider the land around here to be sacred."

With a sense of awe, she considered the artwork that had outlasted the centuries until a slam against the limestone floor brought her back to the present.

Frank was already unloading the mares, so she rushed to help him. Taking care of the horses came first, as usual. This time they stripped off everything but halters. And once they were relieved of their burdens, he attached leads and had her bring them back outside so they could graze, while he hauled his bag and buckets with water.

C.J. secured the mares to a strong pine tree. If only the bats would leave her alone, she would be fine here, she decided, quickly giving the area a once-over. Grass outside the cave was sparse, but the mares picked at it contentedly. And she was relieved to be away from the vertigo-inducing views of the canyon. The torturous landscape had served to remind her that danger lurked around every corner.

As did Frank's reluctance to build a fire, though he protected her against quite a different kind of danger.

"Put on that extra clothing you brought," he told her. "Once we're inside the cave for the night, you'll be plenty warm."

Though she was hardly warm at the moment. And it was going to get much colder. Besides, darkness was quickly descending. But rather than address Frank with emotion, she thought to use logic.

"What about dinner?" she demanded. "How can we cook without a fire?"

He whipped a can of Sterno from one of the pockets in his rucksack. "With ingenuity." He popped the top and lit it with a match.

Frank was nothing if not ingenious. She admired that about the man. Nothing intimidated him. He was the master of his own fate.

But he wasn't invincible, she thought, as she noticed he was limping again.

"Your knee—how is it?"

"Feeling abused, but I'll survive. What about you?"

"Bowlegged. And if I never sit again, it shall be too soon."

She was as good as her word. A quarter of an hour later, layered in warmer clothes, she decided to eat standing up. But when she bent over to get a spoonful of stew, she couldn't help a small groan from escaping her.

"If you feel the need for some massage therapy," Frank muttered, head down, "just say the word."

The thought of his hands on any inch of her body made C.J. choke, but she hurriedly covered by turning the strangled sound into a cough.

"Something went down the wrong way," she murmured.

Though Frank kept his face averted, she could tell he was grinning at her when he said, "Ah-hah. Well, keep in mind that my services are available at any time. I've been told I have magic fingers."

Now he had done it, C.J. thought, her body springing to life the way it had when he'd spooned himself around her to keep her warm. Once more, Frank had lit her imagination. Another night alone with him. Perhaps the need to sleep close again. Her heart thrilled to the thought, for she could feel its furious flutter against her rib cage.

To cover her increasing nerves, she ate nonstop.

"Part of me is going to be sorry to leave this behind," Frank said, giving her an intent look.

A little part of her, as well, C.J. admitted to herself. *This* part. The two of them together. She remembered his saying she would have other guards once he got her to the Quinlan Research Institute. And they would have no real reason to see each other.

But certain that he meant the outdoor challenges that he had bested, she said, "You are an unparalleled man, Frank Connolly."

One about whom she was having odd thoughts unlike any she'd indulged in about other men. Not to mention feelings. Now, *that* was really scary.

After they finished eating and went inside, bringing

the horses with them for the night, she sought a safe topic.

"Do you have any idea of how far we are from the Crow Reservation?"

"Not far from the border, but we're not heading that way."

"I don't understand."

"We're not welcome, for one. That's sacred land, as I said, and we would be trespassing."

"But in our circumstances, surely they would understand and help us."

"No doubt. But truthfully, a couple of off-rez towns are closer than Pryor or St. Xavier up north. I planned on heading straight east."

"To…?"

"Through Custer National Forest. We might come across one of the campgrounds. Or rangers." He handed her a blanket and pillow. "And if not, we'll find the highway on the other side. And eventually one of those towns."

"Highway…towns…what beautiful words." Her eyes widened. "Wait one moment—are you saying that tomorrow is it? The last day we'll be stranded?"

"Hopefully, if nothing else goes wrong."

And then she would be free of the dreaded wilderness. And of him telling her what to do.

So why wasn't she happier?

Exhaustion swept through her, overpowering the call to dangerous speculation.

She set out her blanket and pillow close to his. No padding for them tonight—only the cold, hard limestone beneath them. But Frank had also set one of the saddles at the head of his "bed." He settled against it and from the rucksack surreptitiously removed an object, which he slipped under his blanket before she could see.

A weapon, no doubt.

C.J. shivered at the reminder that mercenaries were after her for her scientific knowledge, and that they needed to remain vigilant until they got to safety.

Frank seemed to have no plans to sleep. Appearing relaxed, his back against the saddle, he seemed content.

"I'll set the flashlight here between us in case you wake," he told her.

"What about you?"

"I'll be right here."

"I mean that you need to sleep also."

"I will."

She didn't believe him. "You think we're in danger now and feel the need to stand guard? I thought that's why we're inside, so no one can find us."

"We're reasonably safe," he said in a tone that convinced her.

"What, then? Is it the nightmares? Are you afraid to sleep?"

"I'm merely unwilling to let down my guard," he countered, his voice soft, his words full of hidden meaning to her ears. "As are you."

"I don't think all the will in the world will keep me awake tonight." Though Frank might have a shot at it.

"That's not what I meant."

"Then what?" she asked.

"Ghosts. I've been trying to deal with mine in the best way I know how for months now, ever since…" He didn't finish. "But you haven't even faced yours."

She'd been correct about his nightmares, then. But what was he intimating about her?

"What ghosts?" she asked.

"The ones you buried when you were eight."

C.J. stiffened. "My parents? They don't haunt me."

"They must or you would be able to talk about them with warmth and maybe a little sadness."

How dare he try to analyze her? In a clipped tone, she said, "I barely remember them."

"You were eight years old," he reminded her. "Not exactly a tot."

Under the covers, she curled her hands into fists. Her short nails had grown sharp and dug into the soft flesh of her palms. "I was still a child."

"A child who shut down inside," Frank said.

He reached over to touch the side of her face, but she pulled away before flesh met flesh, all desire to get closer to him vanquished by his probing words. He dropped his hand if not the subject.

"A child who remained shut down even when she got a new family. And now you're a woman who is still shut down because you feel a need to protect yourself."

"No!"

That indefinable something welled up in her again and beat at the fragile, invisible walls that kept it at bay. Her pulse quickened and she was suddenly having trouble taking a normal breath.

"Coward," he said softly. "You won't even talk about it now. But you need to talk about it, C.J. At the very least, you need to think about it. Resolve what happened in your mind, so that you can be free of the past."

Those invisible walls threatened to crumble. But she wouldn't have it! He couldn't make her mind go where it chose not to.

"You have no right…never mind!"

Irritated beyond words, she jumped up, threw down the blanket and fled toward the mouth of the cave. Privacy, she needed some bloody privacy, where no modern-day Daniel Boone could pry open her head and peer around inside.

"Wait a minute! Where do you think you're going?" Frank asked.

She paused, her back to him. "Outside."

"I'll come with you."

Irritation turning to anger, she whirled around and glared at him. "No, you shan't. I need to be alone for a while!" She enunciated each word. "*If* you don't mind."

Frank gave way. "All right. But take this." He tossed her the flashlight. "And don't go far."

She was already crossing through the mouth of the cave.

Frank called after her. "Be careful!"

Exactly what she intended. Careful enough to get away from him. Who did he think he was, judging her, telling her what she needed to do? He didn't even know her.

A high-pitched yip stopped her short and her breath caught in her throat once more. A series of short yips blended into a lonely howl. Coyote! A second answered. A third. Kin chimed in from other directions. Were they announcing her presence or was that the assumption of an inflated ego? she wondered. Perhaps they didn't even know she was there.

The howling tapered off to that original lone voice. And then nothing.

Darkness and silence surrounded her.

Fighting the willies, C.J. attached her flashlight to a belt loop on her trousers and braved the night air. The chill away from the cave made her suck in her breath, and she hoped that she wouldn't have to venture out again before morning. She persevered, searching for the perfect rock or bush behind which she'd have that needed privacy.

As if anyone were out here to see...

Even as she thought it, a crunch of brush nearby upped her pulse again. Some small creature, no doubt. Perhaps a rabbit or raccoon. No coyote would venture this close to a human. She flashed her light around to make certain.

No movement. No additional sound.

Alone.

Of course she was.

Finally, she found an appropriate bush and made her stop as brief as possible. She was fastening the band of her trousers when she heard it again, the same noise if more defined.

A stealthy footfall?

Her mouth went dry and she whirled around, the light shooting from her hand trembling over the earth. Something flashed through the beam so quickly she barely got an impression. Startled, she faltered backward. A wrong step on an incline jarred her teeth together, and she teetered precariously before coming down wrong and nearly ending on her derriere.

Snapping off the light, she stood and listened, but the only sound was the roar from the inside of her head. Her own breath. Her own heartbeat.

Still, she waited, frozen, aware of the wind picking up, caressing her, leaving icy fingers trailing through every opening in her clothes.

Suddenly the plateau flushed alive with sounds. Skittering, crunching, fluttering. And as the chorus escalated, she snapped on her flashlight. Rather, tried to. It seemed to have died. She endeavored to revive the beam by shaking and snapping and praying.

None worked.

Alone in the dark. No sense of direction. Not so much as a moonbeam to guide her.

She could call out, alert Frank. Once more he would come to her rescue.

But Frank was not on her favored list at the moment, and she wouldn't humiliate herself by whining. Nothing here but nature and her. And if she concentrated, she could retrace her steps and find her way back to the cave.

Concentrate!

Barely breathing, pulse still drumming in her ears, she inched back the way she came. The general direction, anyway, the best she could do.

This was like playing blindman's bluff without the blindfold. Hands out, she felt for obstacles. Rocks. Trees. A bush.

More certain now, she moved faster until her foot hit a dip in the ground. Off balance, she went flying. Her shoulder bounced off one tree and sent her straight into another.

Pushing away from it, she felt something hit her hair. Bats again! She ducked low and beat away the invisible creatures. And then one of her hands brushed something soft and warm.

Something alive? Human?

The touch was fleeting.

Frightening.

Allowing for the humiliation factor, she screamed ''Frank!'' for all she was worth.

Chapter Twelve

"Frank!"

C.J.'s scream startled him from a meditative state to full attention. Frank grabbed his gun from beneath the blanket, then flew through the dark, guided by instincts as efficient as bat radar.

"C.J., where are you?" he called as he burst through the cave entrance.

"Here!"

He honed in on her through the sound of her voice. "Are you all right?"

"Yes, but we may not be alone."

Gun in hand, Frank pulled out an emergency flare from his vest and twisted the cap. An eerie red glow pressed against the blackness of the moonless night. He could see only a limited area around him. Within that perimeter, he and C.J. were the only humans.

A sob of relief escaped her as she ran straight to him, straight into his arms.

"Thank God," she whispered, clinging to him. "Thank God."

Frank wanted nothing more than to drop both flare and gun and to wrap his arms around her. But his natural caution overrode desire.

"What happened?"

"I touched something. Some*one*."

Again he scanned their surroundings as far as the flare allowed. "You're sure? You saw him?"

"No. My flashlight wouldn't work. But I felt something…at least I think I did."

She sounded more panicky than certain. Even so, Frank gave her the benefit of the doubt. Though he concentrated, he had no sense of another presence nearby. Then the wind kicked up with an unearthly howl, and the scene reminded Frank of the scary movies of his childhood.

Had the very elements worked on C.J., forcing her to near hysteria?

"Let's get out of the open."

He pulled her tight against his side and headed straight for the cave. Once there, he pushed her ahead of him through the fissure. Obviously unwilling to let him go, she grasped onto his arm and tugged when he didn't immediately follow.

Instinct prickling the back of his neck, Frank resisted for a moment—was someone really out there or was he now picking up on C.J.'s hysteria? Because he couldn't be certain, he listened hard and stared harder as though his night vision could prick the dark surroundings past the flare's red glow.

But if another Black Order operative *was* in their vicinity, he had the advantage.

So why hadn't he taken C.J.?

An insistent tug on his arm distracted him and he slipped into the cave. C.J.'s fingers were all but biting into his flesh. Her features were drawn taut and she was breathing with difficulty.

"Hey, it's all right," he said reassuringly. "You're all right."

She didn't look all right. Pitiful, really.

Frank couldn't stand letting her be so miserable, so he set down the flare and stuck the gun in his waistband. Then he pulled C.J. into his arms as he'd wanted to do so many times in the past two days. Strictly to offer comfort, he told himself. She trembled against him.

"Cold?" he whispered into her hair. He pulled the golden strands free of the clip and smoothed them over her neck.

She pressed closer. "Hold me, Frank. Just hold me, please."

Tightening his grasp on her, he cupped the back of her neck and head with one hand, then threaded his fingers through the loose hair. She felt so good, so right in his arms. He'd known she would.

Part of him stayed alert. No surprises. But the rest of him gave way to the luxury of having a woman in his arms again. A woman he wanted.

And he was only human, after all, his body reminding him of exactly how human.

"I've never been so scared," she admitted. "Not since I was a child."

"I think the dark and the wind got to you."

"Not just now, tonight. Since Pearl Street Mall. Since I realized that I was in danger. I feel as if we're playing out an extended nightmare."

"You're safe now."

"In your arms, yes. But what about later, when you deliver me to the Quinlan Research Institute? What then?"

"Like I said, you'll have bodyguards."

"I don't want some strange bodyguards, Frank," she said, looking up at him. "I want you."

A vulnerability, a longing in C.J.'s expression got to him and he couldn't resist. Her lips were parted when he covered them with his, and she didn't pull away when he explored the soft crevices of her mouth. Instead, she wrapped her arms around his neck and suckled gently on his tongue, drawing him deeper and deeper inside.

He grew harder, if that were possible, and she rubbed her softness against him. Groaning, he cupped her bottom and spread his legs, then pulled her into him so that she could feel every inch of what she was doing to him.

Her neck arched and she gasped.

Frank almost lost it then. Almost pulled her to the floor of the cave to make love to her. But he couldn't. He had enough sense left to know what was what.

Survival first.

Despite all his reassurances, what if he were wrong and they were being stalked by an invisible enemy? What if that enemy were to strike when they were at their most vulnerable? And how much more vulnerable could they be wrapped up in each other?

He thought it might kill him, but Frank broke the embrace and set C.J. from him.

"We need to keep our heads about us," he said.

"Of course. Our heads."

"Just in case someone is out there. You understand, don't you?"

She backed away from him. "Perfectly."

He could tell she didn't understand. Or didn't want to. She wanted him to comfort her physically, but he couldn't do that and protect her.

And protect her he would, with his own life if necessary. Though hopefully it wouldn't come to that. Hopefully within a day or two tops, he would have her where she belonged. And then, in the rational light of day, with warmth and safety and civilization surrounding them, they would see how they felt about each other.

Frank watched her crawl back under her blanket before settling down himself. In some oblique way, he thought, his mind already drifting, his bringing C.J. to safety would help to make up for his failure in Bosnia.

Not that anything he could do would bring Irina back.

He was hit! The jet spun and then exploded....

He awoke in a hole...the stench of death, of the dying, surrounding him.

Irina of the dark flashing eyes...he ate for her...he existed for her.

"I have to get out of here."

"They're negotiating—"

"Damn their negotiations! I've been here forever."

Waiting...pacing...dying a little more each day he was locked in this hole...

"Only a little more than five months."

"A lifetime."

Her dark eyes searched his...her hand touched his cheek...her lips brushed his.

"I will help you, then. I know someone..."

His chest hurt that she would make such a sacrifice. She would be going against her own people. He cupped her hand in his and kissed her palm tenderly.

She had become his life.

*"What would I do without you? Come with me, Irina.
We can be together where there is no war."*

"Always?" she asked, dark eyes trusting.

"Always."

Always…always…always…

*"Always," he whispered over her lifeless body as he
closed her eyes and kissed her one last time.*

FRANK AWOKE in the dark with a suddenness that left
him breathless and his heart pounding. He listened, but
the woman next to him didn't stir.

He had feelings for her, strong feelings, just as he
had had for Irina. Yet those feelings were as different
as were the women and his relationship with them.

He'd depended on the young Bosnian who had
brought him his food, had practiced her English on
him, had kept him from the kind of loneliness and isolation that would have pushed him out of his mind.
Under circumstances beyond his control, he'd fallen in
love with one of his captors and she with him. To be
truthful, however, he wasn't certain that bond could
have existed in the real world.

Now the roles were reversed. C.J. was dependent on
him. Even so, C.J. was her own woman, not so easily
swayed. This was the real world, *his* world, and Frank
somehow sensed that, if she let herself go, C.J. could
be a perfect fit.

Irina of the beautiful dark eyes and passionate nature—he had loved her, but she was gone and he
couldn't bring her back. He'd felt her with him all these
months, tangled up in his guilt, haunting his dreams,
as if she were still watching over him. As if she were
refusing to leave him while he was still wounded inside. As selfless in death as she had been in life. Per-

haps once he'd proved himself, he could set her spirit free to go on.

And then, he thought, listening to C.J.'s even breathing, he could do the same for himself.

ANOTHER NIGHT OF SLEEPING in fits and starts left C.J. groggy and depressed as they set out from the cave. Frank had left her alone for a while at daybreak, and when he'd returned, he'd reassured her that he'd seen nothing alarming.

And then he'd had nothing much to say to her at all, certainly nothing personal.

A new awkwardness hung between them. Not having experience in matters of the heart—or of the libido— C.J. didn't know what to think or how to act, so she merely withdrew and counted the seconds as they rode off in silence.

She'd never been so miserable. Her hunger was so strident that she swore her navel met her backbone. And every inch of her was sore or bruised…including her heart.

Deep into feeling sorry for herself, C.J. almost ran Double Platinum into Spice Girl. Frank had put up his hand, indicating they should stop, but she hadn't noticed.

She pulled up beside him. "Is something wrong?"

"I'm hoping something's very right." He indicated the cloud of dust a short distance away. "There."

"A vehicle! You're not going to let it get away?"

"Depends…" Frank stared hard for a moment at the dark green vehicle. "Looks like a U.S. Forest Service truck. Let's go for it!"

Frank rode hard, and sore or not, C.J. was determined to keep up with him. And when he waved and yelled, she did the same.

A blare from the truck's horn assured her the driver had seen them. Her spirit lightened. Rescued! They were about to be rescued!

The truck stopped a hundred yards from them. The driver got out. He removed his billed cap from a shock of white hair and waved it. Spirits soaring, C.J. waved back.

They brought the horses up a few yards short of the vehicle. The Forest Service worker stepped out to meet them. He was a little stooped and stiff, probably arthritic, C.J. thought. The way her body was feeling, she certainly could relate.

"You folks lost?" he asked.

"You could say that," Frank agreed, dismounting. "It's a long story, starting with our plane being forced down southeast of here two days ago."

"You're them folks everyone's looking for! Wait till I tell the missus that I'm the one what found you."

"Do you have a cell phone?" Frank asked.

"Nope. Hate the damn things. Don't work in these parts no-how. But I got a radio at the station. Why don't you folks let me take you on down. Dollars to doughnuts you'd appreciate a nice big padded seat instead of them saddles."

Oh, would she!

"I'm not leaving the horses behind," Frank said.

"Don't have to. We can tie 'em to the back of the truck and I'll take it nice and slow so they can follow."

"Sounds good," Frank said, starting toward the horses.

"Let me help you," the man said, following him.

"Hey, you need water," he told C.J., "I got a canteen in the cab."

Her stomach growled. "It's food we need."

"Sorry, can't help you there till we get back to the station." After tying up Spice Girl, he loosened her cinch and checked the load she was carrying. "Got my lunch—a sandwich and apple. Not much, but you're welcome to it."

"It sounds heavenly."

He seemed to be staring at her from behind his dark glasses. "You're not from these parts, are you?"

"England."

"Oh, a far piece from home, then."

"That I am, Mr....?"

"Where are my manners? Harold Bach. But you can call me Hal."

"C. J. Birch," she said, extending her hand, then adding, "and this is Frank Connolly," as he rounded the truck, finished with the horses.

Hal shook hands with them both. "C.J. Frank. Hop in."

A few minutes later, wedged in between the two men, C.J. relaxed against the padded seat that indeed felt wonderful. Hal was as good as his word, going slow enough along the dirt road so that the horses could easily keep up.

"How did you hear about us?" Frank asked.

"Radio. The word went out two days ago. Then yesterday, there was that fella who came looking for you in person."

C.J. felt Frank stiffen beside her. "Who would that be?"

"Said his name was Daniel something."

"Austin?"

"Yup, that'd be the one."

"How the hell would Daniel know to look in this area?"

"He said his people were searching all over the Pryors."

"Foster and Brody, maybe McMurty," Frank muttered. "Not exactly enough bodies to search the entire mountain."

"Surely he has cooperation from other agencies," C.J. said.

"What did this Daniel Austin look like?" Frank asked.

"Tall guy. Blond. Brown eyes." Hal elbowed C.J. "The ladies would find him good-looking, I'm sure."

"Actually, I've never met the man," C.J. said.

No doubt Frank was worried that the man searching for them was a Black Order operative sent to replace the one he'd killed.

"So what happened to your plane to bring it down?" Hal asked.

Frank nudged C.J. and gave her a barely perceptible warning before saying, "It was an old DC-3. One of the engines just died."

Hal whistled. "Musta been something bringing that baby down in one piece."

"It's not exactly in one piece," Frank admitted.

"Still. Me, I never liked planes. Always told the missus if God had meant us to fly, he would have given us wings."

To C.J.'s relief, Hal kept up the friendly conversation all the way down to the station, which was set off the dirt road a ways in a stand of ponderosa pine, making her wonder if they would ever have found it on their own. Probably not. They would have ridden right by.

What luck that Hal happened to be on the road at exactly the right time to meet up with them.

The building was a neat if small log cabin. Not much inside. Two desks, maps and a bulletin board on the wall, a radio on a table.

"We're not fancy here, but at least it's a roof. No indoor plumbing, but if you have a call to nature, you'll find a pump and an outhouse out back." Hal went straight to one of the desks, where he picked up a brown sack. "Here's that lunch I told you about."

"Thank you!"

C.J. was too hungry to worry about calls to nature or anything else at the moment. Ripping the sandwich out of the sack and from its plastic wrap, she handed half to Frank, then savored the first bite.

"I guess I'd better radio the main ranger's station, let 'em know to send someone for you."

"We'd appreciate it," Frank said, moving behind Hal. "We'll need a double horse trailer, as well. The girls have had enough exercise as it is."

"Will do."

As Hal established his contact, C.J. noticed Frank wasn't in as much of a hurry as she to eat. He watched the man fiddle with the radio before so much as taking a bite. Then he looked over the maps of the Pryors and of Custer National Forest, obviously of more interest than food to him.

"...found 'em up near the cave," Hal was saying.

What in the world was Frank finding so fascinating about the maps? C.J. wondered, polishing off her half of the sandwich. Nothing had ever tasted so good. Then he went on to the bulletin board. She eyed the food in

Frank's hand with longing—he didn't seem interested. Perhaps she ought to ask if he would like to share with her.

"Alert those contacts that they're coming in," Hal said.

The half sandwich to his mouth, Frank froze. His gaze was pinned to something on the bulletin board that C.J. couldn't see.

"Will do," the voice on the other end said. *"We'll send someone for them within the hour."*

C.J. took a bite of the apple and noticed that Frank was staring at Hal's back now. She shifted, a sense of unease growing in her as his gaze lowered to Hal's feet and held.

What in the world was bothering him? she wondered.

"C.J.," Frank suddenly said, "why don't you go out and use the facilities first."

"But I..."

The fierce expression he turned on her stopped her from protesting that she didn't have to go.

"...don't want to go alone," she finished lamely, choking down the chewed apple.

"C'mon, you're a big girl."

She looked from Frank, who dropped his sandwich half and put his hands around the back of a wooden chair, to Hal, who was just signing off.

"But there might be a snake around with my name," she said, her heart thundering.

And this time, she wasn't talking about the kind that crawled on the ground. Trusting Frank the way she did, she knew something was terribly wrong.

"Go!" he growled.

But she stayed rooted as he picked up the chair and

brought it down across Hal's back. The legs broke in pieces as easily as matchsticks.

And Hal staggered but didn't go down.

"Frank!"

"Go, dammit!"

Even as Frank yelled, Hal caught himself. Then he straightened, unfolding himself, growing a few inches. And C.J. realized his arthritic condition was a sham. But he was holding himself as if his back were sore…as if a log had dropped across it. The deadfall!

The Black Order mercenary who'd brought down their plane!

When he turned toward Frank, he was holding something metal, something deadly, in his hand.

Click.

A blade sprang free of its housing and Hal rushed Frank, knife arm swinging. C.J. gasped and took a step forward as if she could do something to help.

Frank grabbed the man's wrist and held the knife aloft, yelling, "C.J., get the horses!"

Torn between doing as Frank ordered her and trying to help him—he was now doing a macabre dance with the villain around the office—C.J. chose the first and prayed that she wasn't leaving him to die.

Chapter Thirteen

The bastard was strong, Frank would give him that. Trapped between the man's big body and the desk, he was at a disadvantage. Dark eyes filled with hatred glittered down at him as if they could do the job.

And for a moment, Frank was mesmerized. Something about the man struck a chord in him, almost as if he knew him. And yet he did not.

He didn't know how long he held the mercenary's knife arm suspended before his strength began to give and the point started inching toward him. With his free hand, Frank blindly grabbed for a paperweight he'd seen on the desk. His fingers curled around the rock with many facets. The villain's weapon came closer and closer until the gleam of deadly metal filled his peripheral vision.

It was now or never.

His grip on the rock solid, Frank swung his arm around with maximum force and banged the other man in the lower back, where he knew it would hurt most.

"Aah!"

As planned, the man's shoulders bowed back and his knife arm popped up. Frank swung again, making contact with his wrist this time, so that his grip loosened and he dropped the knife.

Which Frank caught.

"Frank, are you all right?" C.J. called, her voice coming from directly outside the door.

Frank shoved Hal away from him. Uncertain if he could take the bigger man without risk, C.J. being his main concern, he leaned back on a desk and kicked out as Hal rushed forward. He caught the villain in the gut with both feet and knocked the air out of him.

Then Frank got the hell out of there, limping all the way. The kick had started up the knee pain again.

C.J. was already mounted. "Hurry, Frank!" She held Spice Girl's reins out to him.

"Hang on." He lost a precious few seconds by stopping at the truck, where he slashed both front tires with the knife. "That should slow him down."

Frank leaped into the saddle and grabbed the reins from C.J. They took off as the mercenary stumbled outside and yelled after them.

"You're only delaying the inevitable, Connolly! One way or the other, I'll get the woman. And you won't be alive to see what happens to her! I've been waiting for the moment when you draw your last breath, and I won't stop until I take it from you myself!"

Frank clenched his jaw and kept going, making certain that C.J. was able to keep up. Sore she might be, but she was getting a boot-camp introduction to the art of hard riding. She would be an expert by the time they reached her idea of civilization.

The dirt road snaked ahead, but Frank veered off to the east, intending to lose any pursuers in the stands of pines covering Custer National Forest. He wasn't naive. He knew the mercenary was in contact with the

Black Order and could have reinforcements in moments. Reinforcements were already on their way. Thankfully, horses could go where no vehicle could follow, the reason he'd chosen to stick with them rather than chance the truck.

The moment he slowed, C.J. rode up alongside him. "Do you think we'll find one of those campgrounds?"

"If we do, we'll avoid it. Change in plans," Frank explained. "Too dangerous. We don't know how many men he has and how close they might be."

Maybe he should have finished off the mercenary when he'd had the opportunity. Chances were he could have done it...even if he had failed to stop the man with his earlier trap. He'd justified the deadfall thinking that the mercenary would only be hurt, although if he was indeed trying to get his hands on C.J., the man's death would have been deserved.

Truth was, part of him was relieved that he hadn't caused the man's demise. He'd seen enough death and destruction for a lifetime. He hadn't joined Montana Confidential to take lives, rather to save them.

But, Frank thought grimly, he would do whatever he needed to do in order to save C.J.

Whatever it took.

He pushed the horses for a full half hour before feeling safe enough to cool them down and finally stop.

In the midst of a conifer stand so thick that sunlight was all but shut off, no one could see them. And just ahead, an elbow of creek offered a long drink for the horses and a way for him and C.J. to cool off and clean up a bit.

"That was close," he said, dismounting.

Frank took a step and winced. Too bad he couldn't

chance soaking his knee. The cold water of the creek would take down the swelling he felt beneath the wrap.

C.J. dismounted. "You didn't kill our friendly mercenary with your deadfall, after all."

"I didn't even slow him down much."

"Oh, I don't know, he was definitely hurting," she said. "But how did he find us?"

"Probably the old-fashioned way, by tracking us."

"He couldn't keep up with us on foot," she mused. "Perhaps he wasn't on foot."

"Next time I see him, I'll ask," Frank said, keeping a straight face. She did like to analyze things to death.

C.J. merely cocked an eyebrow at him and led her mare to the creek. Frank followed. Standing shoulder to shoulder with her, he thought they made good partners. Maybe they would even make a good couple. In some other life. The longer they were together, the more he realized that he would never want her to go through something like this again.

"What could he have against you?" C.J. suddenly asked.

He knew she was thinking about the threat the mercenary had thrown after them.

"I wish I knew. When he had me pinned with that knife, I felt his hatred was personal. And that I should know why. That I should know *him*..."

"Perhaps you do. You've been living a very dangerous life. Maybe you met him in the military."

Frank shook his head. "No. We've never met."

"How can you be so certain? He said something about having waited a long time," C.J. reminded him. "And he looks different every time we see him."

"True enough."

And something to think about.

Perhaps if he went over those last few years he spent in the military, it would come to him. It's just that he'd been doing his very best to forget.

"How *did* you know something was wrong earlier?" she asked. "What made you suspect he wasn't really some guy named Hal?"

"The radio frequency he was using, for one. I saw a list of Forest Service contacts on the bulletin board—he was using the other end of the frequency. And then the boots were a dead giveaway."

"What about his boots?"

"He was wearing zippered paratrooper boots. Very distinctive, with the zipper closure on the side so you don't have to lace them. The same pair I saw on our rent-a-pilot. I have a pair myself, probably the reason I noticed."

"Thank heaven you did."

When she turned her gaze on him, the look she gave him gripped Frank's chest so hard it hurt. Within the mix of admiration and relief he read something more—a vulnerability that he was certain had to do more with him than with their situation.

What in the world was he going to do about her?

GILAD SEETHED as he changed back into his own clothes. He was getting sick of the game, yet it played on despite his best efforts. He should have finished it the night before, outside the cave, but grabbing the woman in the dark wouldn't have been much of a challenge. And it wouldn't have taken care of Connolly.

Besides, he wasn't one to cry uncle, and he still had a card to play.

Soon though, the bodies would be found—the two

rangers and the worker whose clothing he'd borrowed. Once that happened, the manhunt for him would be on.

Try to get a job done then with all the government drones scurrying around looking for clues!

The sound of engines approaching alerted him. A quick look out the window assured him that members of the Black Order had arrived.

Picking up his bag of tricks, Gilad steeled himself and left the cabin.

Tall, square, dark bristling mustache in a naturally bronzed face, the man named Nizam jumped from the first vehicle and approached him. Other men got out but kept their distance and waited for orders.

Not bothering to hide his contemptuous expression, Nizam asked, "Is Dr. Birch inside?"

"I'm afraid not."

"You let her go again?"

Gilad gave Nizam a sly smile. "If you and your men had been deemed able to do the job by the head of the operation, my services wouldn't have been necessary."

"As I see it, you're a waste of money."

Gilad acted so fast the bigger man never saw it coming. In less than three seconds, he had the prick pressed up against the hood of the Jeep, a knife at his throat.

Not his favorite knife—Connolly had kept that one after immobilizing him—but it would do. And he would get the switchblade back.

"Don't tempt me," he said, aware of the men spreading around behind him.

One of them hissed, "Nizam—"

"Stay back!" Gilad ordered. "Or I'll gladly cut his throat."

"Keep back," Nizam agreed. "All right, all right, you've proved your point. Now let me up." When Gilad didn't immediately comply, he said, "We're both on the same side, you maniac!"

Which made Gilad laugh. He wasn't on any side but his own. Nevertheless, he did back off.

Nizam rubbed his neck. "What next? Are you going to keep tracking them on that mountain bike?"

The mountain bike he'd brought in the plane had served him well. But he'd had enough of the thing and had ditched it gladly when he'd appropriated the truck.

"No need," he said. "I have their coordinates at any given time. When I'm ready, I'll go right for them."

"How?"

"By using my backup plan. Perhaps you've heard of those?" he asked sarcastically. "They left, but with a present from me. A transmitter."

Which he'd put in place when helping secure the horses to the back of the truck.

"My men and I are ready," Nizam said. "Say the word and we're after them."

"No 'we' about it!" Gilad growled. "If you know what's good for you, you won't interfere until I call for you again. They're mine!"

Most especially Connolly. He'd kill any man that touched the bastard before him. Taking the pilot's life himself was a matter of honor, and in this, he would not be denied.

With that, he commandeered the Jeep, leaving eight men to pile in the second vehicle any way they could.

THE PAVED ROAD CAME upon them with a suddenness that left C.J. disbelieving.

"A mirage," she murmured, stopping the palomino several yards short of the path to civilization.

"It's real, all right."

"No autos, though."

"We're not in the heart of civilization yet," Frank said. "But we are getting there."

"So you keep saying."

But this time he was correct. Less than five minutes later, a pickup sped by, the dogs in the back the only parties seemingly interested in two people on horse-back. A short while later, an eighteen-wheeler passed them. And then some teenagers in an old beater who whooped at them but didn't stop.

Another five minutes, two more cars and a pickup, and C.J. could see something ahead that looked like a town.

She didn't care that there was only a handful of buildings or that they were sadly in need of repair. It was a real town with real people and real telephones and real food!

"We made it," she murmured.

"Did you have any doubts?"

She gave Frank a fake glare—she was too happy to be cross because he was teasing her.

A hundred yards later, they passed a sign announcing the town limits.

Elk Valley, Population 143

But the two-block-long town ahead couldn't possibly hold that many people, C.J. thought as they got closer. The one hundred and forty-three citizens had to include nearby ranchers, as well.

On quick inspection, she noted the Sleepy Traveler Motel with its two gas pumps out front, the Pennywise Convenience Store, the Grizzly Bar and—eureka!—the Hungry Man Café.

"Food!" she said, her stomach growling.

"But first we have to—"

"—see to the horses." A familiar refrain, she thought. "I know. I know."

They couldn't exactly leave them to wander around town alone. But imagining she smelled food, C.J. was certainly tempted.

A young woman coming out of a store looked their way. Her dark eyes went wide at the sight of them walking their horses down what C.J. figured would be colorfully called Main Street.

Frank waved at her. "Excuse me. Is there a stable around here?"

"Uh, not exactly."

"We need a place to leave our horses."

"Marvin Pritchard's place runs right to the far edge of town." She waved that way without taking her eyes from them. "He might be able to help you."

"Thanks, ma'am," Frank said, tipping his brimmed hat. "The faster we get there," he said to C.J., goosing his horse into a slow trot, "the faster you eat."

His mood had lightened considerably, as had her own. Free at last of the bloody wilderness—what more could a city-loving scientist ask for? Not that Elk Valley could be called a city by any stretch of the imagination.

As they moved down its single street, she realized it was a town barely holding on.

Thankfully, Mr. Pritchard was more than willing to board the horses for a day or two. Probably he could use the extra money Frank offered. The elderly rancher said that he would take care of the tack, then water and feed the mares before letting them out into the pasture.

The only think Frank took was his rucksack. For some reason, he was reluctant to part with it.

Then it was to the Hungry Man Café, nearly empty

as it wasn't even dusk yet. According to Frank, ranchers and hands would be out working their spreads for another hour or two. Which meant they would get fast service, C.J. thought with anticipation.

After they used the facilities to freshen up, Frank escorted her to a booth at the windows. A small vase of flowers fronting the salt and pepper and sugar dispensers made C.J. smile. She sat on one side of the table, while he dumped his bag on the other bench.

"I'm gonna send out a loud and clear SOS," he told her, indicating a wall phone. "Would you mind ordering for both of us?"

"Of course I will. Anything in particular you want?"

"Yeah, foo-ood!"

C.J. grinned as he headed for the telephone. She didn't care what she ate, either, she thought, taking a quick look at the menu.

A red-haired waitress carrying a pot stopped at the booth. "Coffee, honey?"

"Tea, please."

A dark eyebrow lifted, but the woman merely asked, "What about your man?"

Her man? *Frank?*

An odd feeling filling her, she said, "Um, you'll have to ask him."

The waitress put down the coffeepot and took out her order pad. "So what's your fancy?"

"Steaks. For both of us," C.J. added. "Mashed potatoes, carrots and salads. And soup to start. And then dessert. Do you have anything chocolate?"

"Cake? Pie?"

"Both."

Both dark eyebrows arched this time. "Sounds like you're hungry."

"You have no idea."

But as hungry as she was, C.J.'s enthusiasm for food was dampened a bit, not at the thought of being rescued, of course, but at the thought of being separated from Frank.

Free of Frank Connolly at last—now, why didn't that feel better than it did?

Attraction might be rife between them, but that was all they had in common. They couldn't be more different, C.J. reminded herself.

She was dedicated to her work. To the scientific principles. To a cause minus the people involved. To things she understood. Frank was centered on nature and on people, and C.J. didn't know if she could relate to him away from this unique and forced isolation that they'd shared for a few days.

Isolation in her laboratory would be a welcome relief from all the emotions that this unsuitable man had wrought in her.

Which was sensible of her to realize.

For once she was safely ensconced at the Quinlan Research Institute, who knew if she would ever see Frank Connolly again?

"Do you think they've found Frank yet?"

Whitney threw an arm around Jewel's shoulders. "I don't know, honey, but I'm sure that Daniel will call and let us know what's going on at the first opportunity."

They'd been out riding together. Whitney had suggested it to get the girl's mind off the search and rescue for a while—about the only positive contribution she could think of making—but it hadn't worked. The whole time they were out it had been *Frank this* and *Frank that.* The poor darling had it bad, Whitney feared. Having had an inappropriate crush of her own at just about the same age, she empathized.

"I think I'm gonna see to Silver before coming in," Jewel said.

"I'm sure he'll appreciate the attention."

And Whitney would have the house to herself for a while. Dale McMurty had gone to town for groceries and had taken little Molly with her. So Whitney could relax for a while without someone frowning at her as if she were doing something wrong just by being alive.

Maybe she would take a bubble bath, she thought, already dreaming of relaxing in the claw-footed tub, bubbles up to her chin. She could use the time to pore through the catalogs she'd found in a rack in the living area.

But the moment she stepped into the house, the telephone rang and all thoughts of catalogs dissolved like bubbles against water.

Even though she expected to hear Daniel's voice, she answered, "Lonesome Pony. This is Whitney."

"And this is Frank Connolly."

"Omigod!" Her heart skipped a beat. "You're all right! Everyone's been so worried. Where are you?"

"A town called Elk Valley."

"And Dr. Birch?"

"She's with me and in one piece. Can you get Daniel to the phone?"

"He's not here. He's out looking for you. They started for the crash site before light this morning."

"They—you mean the boys?"

"Kyle and Court and Patrick," she said.

"Damn! Does Daniel have his cell phone with him?"

"Yes, but he may be out of range as he was when I tried to reach him earlier."

"That's the trouble with cell phones. One of them, anyway."

Whitney thought quickly—finally, something she could contribute to the situation.

"I'm not real familiar with the Montana roads yet, so if you can give me an idea of how to find you, I can drive out right now and be at Elk Valley as fast as I can."

A long pause made her excitement wane.

"It, uh, might be better if we waited for Daniel or one of the boys...you not knowing the roads and all."

Of course it would. He didn't even consider her competent enough or perhaps trustworthy enough to drive her SUV to pick him up and bring him home.

"Yeah, sure," she said, the back of her throat thick with familiar disappointment. "By the way, we identified that rent-a-pilot on your flight. His name is Gilad. People call him the Masqued Mercenary because he takes on different identities. But I guess you already know something about that."

"I got that idea," Frank agreed.

"Gilad is considered very, very dangerous, and he'll be on your tail, so watch out for him. He could be anyone."

"Thanks, Whitney. If you hear from Daniel or one of the others soon," Frank said, "tell them we're at the Hungry Man Café. The number here is 555-7463."

"Got it." She grabbed a pen and scribbled down the number on the pad next to the telephone. "You sit tight. Don't go anywhere without letting me know first."

"I'll do my best to keep you informed."

Whitney frowned at his sarcastic tone. But before she could call him on it, he hung up. She wasted no time in trying to reach Daniel. But no soap. He wasn't anywhere his cell phone could get a signal.

Why couldn't Frank Connolly have just let her come get him and Dr. Birch?

Invading Daniel's office, she pulled out his Montana map and found the town about thirty miles south of Billings.

"C'mon, Daniel, call. You're so close...."

Frustrated more than ever, Whitney was ready to shop.

FRANK COULD HARDLY BELIEVE that so much food could disappear into so slender a woman. C.J. finished her food, and then, when he'd had enough and pushed his plate away, she finished his, as well. Not to forget the double dessert she'd demolished, both chocolate.

He likened her to a squirrel packing it in for the coming winter. Undoubtedly, she feared their situation, imagined that they would be on the run again and without acceptable food.

She needn't worry, though. They were almost home free. Almost.

"That phone does ring, doesn't it?" he asked the waitress when she gave him the bill.

"Well, it doesn't whistle Dixie, honey."

"Just checking."

"I can't believe the MacNair woman hasn't heard from the other agents yet," C.J. said after the waitress walked away to wait on a new customer. "It's been dark for some time now. They can't still be searching, so where could they be?"

"My best guess is that they got on the trail and decided to stay on it, pick it up again at first light. At least, that's what I would do."

"And relish it," she murmured.

Frank heard the disapproval in her low tone. For a woman who hated the great outdoors, she was getting along fine, despite all her complaints.

From his wallet, he fished out enough money to cover the bill and give the waitress a generous tip.

"I don't know about you, but I could use some rest."

"The Sleepy Traveler?"

"You read my mind."

Frank handed the waitress the money and asked her to direct any calls for him over to the motel. He figured he could call Lonesome Pony for an update—should there be one—once he was settled in his room.

They trudged toward the motel. C.J. seemed to drag her feet and to have to force her eyes to stay open. She yawned and burped simultaneously.

"Was it as good the second time around?" he asked.

She merely snorted in response.

And Frank fought the urge to put an arm around her shoulders and pull her close. Getting away from her for a few hours would be good for his psyche. Sleep would allow him to see their situation with a new clarity.

For the past few days, they'd been too dependent on each other. It was only natural that forced isolation together had brought them unnaturally close.

In their real lives, they would have nothing in common. They might be friendly acquaintances, but nothing more. And they would be back to their real lives soon. He would go on from one dangerous situation to another, while C.J. would be safe, cocooned in her laboratory.

Just as it should be, he decided.

The neon motel sign was having fits. Below its flickering light in the parking lot stood five hulks—all eighteen-wheelers. Truckers had pulled in for the night.

The motel office was seedy, which didn't bode well for the rooms. He was too tired to care, but C.J. might be another story. So, when he saw a particularly big bug crawl along the boot-stained carpeting, he kept it to himself.

A man with a bright red crew cut and wearing horn-rimmed glasses with lenses thick enough to distort his eyes popped up from behind the counter. "Can I help you folks?"

"I sure hope so."

The clerk grinned, his buckteeth showing. "You two are in luck. We have one room left with lots of special features—our honeymoon suite."

Chapter Fourteen

"This may not be the Taj Majal, but at least it's not out in the open," C.J. said, looking around at the honeymoon suite.

The room was as shabby as the motel's exterior. The red satin coverlet on the heart-shaped bed was frayed, as were the cloth shades over the cupid lamps framing it. Looking up, she gawked at the ceiling mirror over the bed.

"You're right—you wouldn't find all this outside. I wonder what supposedly makes this a suite," Frank mused. "The love seat?"

C.J. glanced at the small fringed couch crowded into a corner. "That and the luxurious dining area." A tiny table and two spindly legged chairs. "So it's in bad taste. But after what we have encountered, this looks lovely to me. And a shower sounds like heaven. Why don't you go first? I'll get some ice for your knee."

"I can do that," Frank insisted. "I don't want you out there alone in the dark."

"This isn't a cave and there are no bats to fight off."

"You might be surprised at the wildlife around here. So stay inside."

His tone brooked no argument. But C.J. was tired of

taking orders. She had always depended on herself—
up until the last few days.

"You cannot tell me what to do every moment,"
she said more calmly than she was feeling. "If I want
to take a walk and get some ice, then I shall. And I
do!"

Frank leaned against the door. "You'll have to get
by me first."

"I was going to try to make your knee better, not
worse," she threatened.

"You would hurt the man who saved your hide, and
more than once, may I add?"

The reminder made her try reasoning with him.
"Please, Frank, stop being so stubborn. We're safe
now. This Gilad person can't possibly find us this
quickly. No hoofprints outside the motel. So just step
away from the door."

"All right, but we'll go to the ice machine together."

"I'm an adult, not a child. I don't need you to hold
my hand!" As much as she might like it. "Shower.
And don't use all the hot water."

"We could solve that problem by showering together."

"I think not."

Her imagination stirred, anyway. Though he hadn't
moved from the door, C.J. grabbed the room key and
ice bucket and faced him down. For a moment, she
thought he would impose his considerable will on her.
And then he stepped aside.

"Be careful out there."

She wouldn't put it past him to follow her. But the
door closed behind her and stayed closed.

The ice machine was located at the far end of the

building. Paranoia having set in the night before, C.J. was aware of every night sound around her. At least the moon was out, lending an eerie silver glow to the parking lot. If there should be any movement between the trucks, she would be able to spot it.

But all remained still.

It was almost too quiet, as if the night were holding its breath.

Rubbing the raised flesh from her arms, C.J. hurried the last dozen yards.

The ice machine sat between two vending machines. She'd never been one for sodas. But the chocolate bars in the other machine made her mouth water. She was indeed a dyed-in-the-wool chocoholic. Unfortunately, she had no change or one dollar bills.

Frank did, though.

What irony—if only she had let him accompany her, she could have let him buy her all the candy bars she could stuff in her pockets. Not that she would ever tell him.

Taking the lid from the ice bucket, she began to fill it. Beyond the noise of falling ice cubes, she heard something else. Her pulse tripped and she released the lever to listen.

Footsteps.

And they were coming toward her.

Her breath caught in her throat and she whipped around as a man rolled up behind her.

He punched the glasses up his nose. "Getting refreshments?" the motel clerk asked.

"Ice. Just ice."

The clerk stepped over to the vending machine and started inserting coins. "Got thirsty and I hate coffee."

"Oh." Her pulse steadied.

The bucket was not yet full. Not enough ice to pack around Frank's knee. So C.J. turned back to the machine and pressed the bucket under the opening. As cubes dropped down, she realized the clerk was eyeing her surreptitiously.

Making her nerves stretch taut anew.

Why was he so interested in her? she wondered, suddenly remembering that Gilad was a master of disguise.

He had appeared as a statue, a Hispanic pilot and as an older and arthritic man. Why not a nerd? The motel clerk was tall enough, broad enough to be Gilad....

C.J. only hoped she hadn't fooled herself into thinking they were finally safe.

The bucket was full. She would have to turn her back on him now.

"Good night," she said, backing away instead.

"Sleep tight," he returned, snickering to himself. "Don't let the bed bugs bite."

C.J. whipped around and scurried along the building, aware of him following.

What if he attacked her?

A weapon—what could she use? All she had was the ice. She could throw the ice at him. Right, that would stop him long enough so he could shake the chill away.

Fumbling for the key in her pocket, C.J. realized she could use that as a weapon. If he came at her, she could poke his eye out...before he did something worse to her.

Practically sprinting to the honeymoon suite, she unlocked the door and popped it open, ready to yell for Frank, assuming he could hear her above the pounding of the shower.

The man was upon her.

C.J. flipped around, her back to the open doorway, the ice bucket before her.

The clerk punched at his glasses again as he continued on his way to the motel office.

Leaving C.J. weak-kneed and shaking as she slid into the room and dead-bolted the door behind her.

YOU WOULD THINK a big plastic bag of ice could cool a man down.

Frank cursed the Fates that he wasn't so lucky. Half lounging across the love seat, he had propped his legs on one of the spindly chairs. The makeshift ice bag enveloped his right knee...for all the good it did him.

In the bathroom, the shower was pounding C.J., who was singing to herself. She had a nice voice. Lovely. As lovely as the lady herself.

That was his problem. Thinking about C.J., water spilling over her head, rivulets pouring wet channels through the soap laving her soft skin. Sweat trickled down his spine. He only had himself to blame, of course, suggesting as he had that they shower together to save on hot water.

While he'd been showering, he'd imagined it all.

Running both hands over her breasts, his fingers lightly playing with her nipples until they hardened into nubs. Trailing his palm down her belly until he reached the protected area between her thighs. Her opening for him and his preparing her until she sobbed for him to take her. He'd imagined the taking part, too, against the shower wall, her clinging to his neck and lifting herself to wrap her legs around his waist. Him burying himself in her.

The fantasy clung to him, tortured him, lascivious

thoughts keeping him hot and bothered despite the sack of ice that was supposed to make him feel better.

Maybe he ought to move it elsewhere, he thought grimly, or he would never sleep.

Suddenly he realized the shower had stopped. Maybe there would be some relief for him yet. But it didn't come quickly and it didn't take. The moment she stepped out of the bathroom, head turbaned in a towel, her shirt clinging to her damp skin, the problem renewed itself.

He wanted her and the bordello-like atmosphere of the room wasn't helping his situation.

"What are you doing there?"

"Icing my knee as you ordered."

"No, I mean on the love seat."

"Trying to get comfortable."

"You would be more comfortable on the bed."

No, he wouldn't, Frank thought, but he said, "I wanted you to enjoy the bed."

"Well, I won't enjoy it alone. I—I mean knowing that you're stuck on that thing. You don't even fit."

"It'll do."

"Frank, don't be stubborn, please. Just get into bed. It's plenty big enough for us both."

"But—"

"No buts." She turned back the red cover. "Come on now, get off that thing and over here so we can get to sleep."

Figuring she would argue him to death if he didn't do as she wanted, Frank complied. She certainly could be stubborn enough when she chose to. He made a detour to the bathroom, where he dumped the ice in the sink.

When he returned to the bedroom, she was watching

him intently from the edge of the bed. "How's the knee?"

"The *knee?* The knee is better, thanks." Even if other parts of him weren't.

"You don't seem to be limping. That's an improvement."

Frank grunted his agreement as he carefully settled in on the other side of the bed. One of the cupid lamps illuminated the room. Enough light for him to see their reflections in the mirror above. He shut his eyes against the fantasies that might inspire, but he didn't need visuals to stimulate his imagination.

"Good night, Frank." C.J.'s murmur was followed by a sharp click.

"Night."

He peeked into the darkness. She'd shut off Cupid, but he could hear her soft breathing, could imagine that warm air against his ear stir things inside him.

Disgruntled, Frank turned his back to her and hiked himself onto his side. The bed whirred to life under him for a few seconds.

"What was that?" C.J. asked.

"Weird springs?"

But when Frank turned back and tested the mattress by throwing his weight on it, the same thing happened. And then he heard C.J. move and the whole bed shuddered.

"A vibrating bed!" Frank said. "Of course the honeymoon suite would have a vibrating bed!"

He experimented. Every time he made a sharp movement, it set off the mechanism.

"How does anyone sleep through that?" C.J. asked, clicking on Cupid.

"I don't think sleep is the point." When she continued to look puzzled, he said, "Just the opposite."

"Oh..."

Frank got off the bed and looked around for some kind of control box. If there was one in the room, it eluded him. He then searched the wall for the plug, but the bed seemed to be hardwired underneath.

"Frank, at this rate, you won't get any sleep."

"You've got that right."

"No, I mean get back into bed and settle down," she said. "As long as we don't actually move around too much, nothing will happen."

Except in his imagination.

He dropped onto the bed. It vibrated merrily as if welcoming his return.

"I guess this is one of those special features the clerk thought we would enjoy."

C.J. snorted.

Frank glanced at her and thumped his pillow. Hard. The bed hummed.

Laughter erupted from her.

Admitting it was pretty amusing, Frank had to grin. He settled back into the mattress, which had indeed quieted down.

She turned and bounced her hip against it. The motor sprang to life once more, throwing them both into a fit of laughter.

"Yeah, we're going to get sleep, all right."

"We will, we will."

C.J.'s mouth was split into a Cheshire grin and Frank thought he'd never seen anything more beautiful. She was relaxed—really relaxed—as if she believed at last that everything would be all right.

And perhaps everything would work out, Frank

thought, as she reached over and shut off Cupid once more. He realized that he was relaxed as well.

Laughter was good for the soul.

As was sleep.

HE WAS HIT!

He awoke in a hole...the stench of death surrounding him.

Irina of the dark flashing eyes...

"I have to get out of here...I've been here forever."

Waiting...pacing...dying a little more each day he was locked in this hole...

"I know someone. My brother. You just have to be patient."

"How patient? How much longer?"

He couldn't stand much more of this.

"I—I don't know. He's gone underground for some time now, but I'll get a message to him somehow, Frank, and he'll help me get you out, I know he will."

"Come with me, Irina. We can be together where there is no war."

Always...always...always...

THE MATTRESS QUAKING and a hoarse "Irina, no-o-o!" startled C.J. awake. Her heart thundered until she realized Frank was having another of his nightmares and had set off the vibrator again.

"Frank, Frank, wake up," C.J. murmured, turning on the bedside light.

She checked the time. Almost dawn.

"How could you allow this? How?" he gasped.

He was in the throes of something so distressing that it bowed his spine and distended his features even in sleep.

Irina. Something had happened to a woman he obviously cared about, perhaps loved. Bad enough that Frank had been shot down and held prisoner...

C.J. gently touched his shoulder and murmured nonsense to him, as one would to calm an anguished child or a frightened animal.

Gradually, her touch and the sound of her voice filtered through his nightmare, for his body relaxed and his breathing calmed and, thankfully, oh, thankfully, the bed stopped its raucous vibrating.

Until he sat straight up, that was. But this time the hum died as quickly as it began.

"What...?" He blinked against the soft light. "Oh, God, not again!" He buried his face in his hands.

C.J. reached out to touch him comfortingly, but stopped, her hand inches from his arm. "Would you like to talk about it?" She pulled herself back together. "I can be a good listener."

"I already told you. I was shot down and held as a prisoner of war."

"But you didn't tell me about Irina."

He met her steady gaze. A moment stretched between them. His agony was so sharply etched in his eyes that C.J. felt it pierce her own heart.

"She helped me escape," he said. "And for that, she died."

C.J. reached out again and this time put her hand over his. "You feel responsible."

"I *am* responsible. She wanted me to wait for her brother but I couldn't stand the isolation, the cries in the night, the stench of death any longer. I grew impatient and pushed her into acting without him, even though she'd gotten a message through to him. She was young. Inexperienced in subterfuge."

"But she loved you."

"Yes."

As he must have loved her, C.J. thought.

"One of the guards had become suspicious of her. He must have sensed there was more between us than prisoner and jailer. He said he watched her movements closely, and that night he…he called her a traitor and shot her. I killed him for it, but that didn't save her. I couldn't save her. I promised she would always be with me. I lied."

"You didn't lie. She *is* with you."

C.J. could see that. She could understand why he'd fallen asleep on her the other night. And why he'd pushed her away in the midst of comforting her. Of course. He was in love with another woman.

With a memory, she amended. With a beautiful ghost who had given her life for him.

Frank would never forget Irina, C.J. knew. She would be part of him always, just as he had promised her. Buried deeply inside so far that eventually he might not even think of her often. But she would be there just the same.

Her eyes filled with tears for him, and without thinking, she crawled over the few feet separating them. The mattress seemed to hiccup a few times before it settled down again. Her hip wedged against his, her arms curled around his neck and their foreheads lightly touched.

He was breathing hard, his body rigid, his attitude unreceptive.

Though not experienced in dealing with people on a personal level or in offering comfort, she was willing to do whatever she could for the man who had saved her life, had protected hers with his, even if it meant drawing pain from the very center of her being and exposing it.

Pain that she had hidden or ignored for most of her life.

Pain whose very existence she had denied.

"I think about my birth parents more than I want to admit," she murmured. "I try not to, but sometimes I can't stop the memories from overcoming me. I couldn't save them, so why didn't I die with them?"

His arms encircled her in response. Emotions welled in her throat like a huge, impassible lump.

"Because it wasn't your time, just as it wasn't mine," he said. "Your parents wouldn't have wanted you to die, C.J., no more than Irina would have wanted me to die. But being the one left behind, it's hard not to feel guilty."

Frank slid a hand up her back and rested it on her neck. His fingers spread and cradled the back of her head.

It felt so good, she thought. So very, very good.

"You can't forget something that breaks your heart," he whispered into her hair. "So you shouldn't try."

They had that in common. Two broken hearts, hers for the mother and father she had barely begun to know, his for the love of his life.

She had discerned from the beginning that this George Clooney-handsome man was not for her, C.J. thought sadly. She wasn't going to fool herself into thinking that what had been flaring between them since they'd first met was more than simple animal attraction.

Or at least that's all it must be for him.

Still, she held on tighter.

Frank's warmth crept into her, binding her to him.

Gradually, she noted his breathing grew easier and his body seemed to meld with hers so that she couldn't tell where hers ended and his began. Even their hearts seemed to beat in unison.

She pulled her head back so that she could look into his face. Really, really look. She wanted to memorize every inch of Frank Connolly—he was one person who'd entered her life that she never, ever wanted to forget.

He knuckled the hair back from her cheek. Her lids fluttered in response to the exquisite touch.

"You're so very beautiful," he murmured.

Her lips curled into a smile and she countered, "I'm a scientist."

"Science is highly underrated."

His gaze flared and so did she.

He kissed her. A demand rather than a request, she thought hazily, responding with all her heart.

His fingers tangled in her hair and he dipped her, then shifted position so he lay over her and set the bed in motion. The hum of the mattress had new meaning now. Her lower body rocked provocatively, and against her, matching hers hip to hip, his did as well.

Excitement filled her at the knowledge that Frank Connolly wanted her and he wanted her now.

But was it really her, Cecilia Jane Birch, whom he wanted? a little voice asked.

Perhaps he really wanted Irina. After the nightmare, after what he'd told her, she realized he had to be thinking about his lost love.

She didn't want to be a substitute, C.J. thought hazily as a syrupy heat rose from her center. She didn't want to be a surrogate for a dead woman. And yet...she wanted to lie with Frank Connolly more than anything she had wanted in her life, with the exception of wanting to save her parents, at which she had failed miserably.

An impasse.

This had never happened to her before. She'd never related to anyone the way she did to Frank. She'd never before felt so thoroughly seduced, mind and heart as well as body. For in addition to alternately irritating her and making her feel safe, Frank managed to pull from her all the things she'd kept buried for so long.

Wishes…longing…a feeling of connection.

They weren't out of danger, she reasoned, as he ran lips and teeth down her throat and into the deep V of her blouse. No one was coming to their rescue yet. For all she knew, this could be her last night on earth. Gilad could find and kill them in their beds.

The bottom line: she didn't want to die a virgin.

He pushed aside the material with his mouth and latched onto the flesh below. The curving plump flesh of a very sensitive breast. A sound issued from the back of her throat and C.J. arched into his mouth. His tongue dipped below the lace of her bra and caught her nipple, which immediately tightened and sent a shock wave throughout her body.

Frank was the first man she had ever truly, wholeheartedly wanted, and C.J. feared that she would never again experience this passion.

Once was better than not at all, she reasoned, exploring him with shaky hands.

She had never before touched a man so intimately…had never before heard the quickening of a man's breath because of her…had never before longed for a man to strip her clothes anyway, as if they were an impediment to be overcome.

Too many nevers in her life, she thought hazily. Then, as if her thinking it had made it so, their clothing magically disappeared, an article at a time, until they lay naked in each other's arms, kissing and touching as if they were meant to be together.

His palm felt hot against her belly as he inched downward. And when he fingered her open and laved her with her own wetness, she felt hotter. She gripped his back, wanting more, wanting to know true intimacy with another human being.

Once was better than not at all, she told herself again as he shifted and wedged himself between her thighs, his engorged flesh dipping into the entrance of her wet center.

She could live with once. She could live with his needing another woman and still take comfort in him and let him take comfort in her.

She opened to him and he slid inside until nature stopped him. But she arched, dug her fingers into his back, urged him to go farther.

Once...just once.

He pushed through her barrier and she cried out in pain and in the promise of something brighter. He took it slow, kissing her, stroking her inside and out, assaulting her most sensitive spots until that promise was fulfilled. An unnamed restlessness filled her. A need so deep that she felt she might drown in the passion.

Once, just once, she wanted to experience being a woman fulfilled.

And then, if it came to that, she could die happy.

Chapter Fifteen

The roar of an engine rumbling to a start woke Frank and shook the room. A truck, he thought, opening his eyes. Rays of gray from the blinds breached the darkness. Dawn and the start of another day on the run.

Still sleepy and somewhat disoriented, he lay staring up at the mirror and at the nude woman sleeping against his side. A warmth swirled through him as he remembered how full of surprises Dr. C. J. Birch had been.... A virgin...he should have guessed. He almost felt guilty...almost. How could he when what had happened between them had been so right.

Another engine—this one of slighter capacity—pulled up. And a horn honked repeatedly.

Gently lifting C.J.'s arm so as not to disturb her sleep, Frank ducked under it and off the bed, careful not to induce more vibrating. He stepped into his briefs and undershirt on his way to the window.

"...know where...find...clerk?" came the muffled bits of a question. "...not...office."

Frank peered through the blinds.

One of the eighteen-wheelers was about to roll out. The trucker was hanging out of the cab talking to a man Frank couldn't see, because the guy's Jeep blocked his line of sight. The trucker pointed toward the vending machines, and the other man climbed back into his vehicle and drove off in that direction.

"C.J., wake up," Frank said, already gathering his clothes from the floor.

She groaned as if she weren't ready to face the day. Well, she had to be ready!

"C.J., now! Come on. Get up and get dressed and hurry!" he ordered.

Practically flying off the bed before seeming to realize she was naked, C.J. scrambled for her shirt and pulled it on as if she were embarrassed. The mattress vibrated—a reminder of the night before—but died down quickly.

Frank couldn't believe she was having trouble looking at him. After what they'd shared, after exploring every part of each other's bodies and hearts, he didn't know how she could feel anything but comfortable with him. Maybe he shouldn't have yelled, but the situation had him pumped.

"W-what's going on?" Hands shaking, she was doing her best to button the shirt.

He averted his gaze so he wouldn't be distracted by her more charming attributes. "We have to get out of here and fast."

She practically choked. "Gilad?"

"I don't know, but I'm not taking any chances."

Her sharp nod told him she was on track. From the corner of his vision, he could see her pulling on her panties and trousers. He gave her his full attention as she pulled on her jacket. Only then did she find her bra. Wavering for a second, she stuck it in her pocket and got to her footwear.

Already wearing his boots, Frank dug into his ruck-sack and pulled out a mirror before going to the door.

"What are you doing?"

"Checking on our chances to get out the front way without being seen."

Which were slim to none.

For in the mirror that he furtively stuck out between door and frame, he could see the back of the driver outside the Jeep. He was talking to the bucktoothed clerk, who was nodding and brandishing a can of pop.

If he wasn't mistaken, that can was waggling in their direction!

"How the hell did he find us this fast?" Frank muttered, thinking quickly.

C.J. was finger-combing her hair as he flew by her and into the bathroom. The window was a bit high, but it looked big enough for him to squeeze through.

"In here," he said, climbing into the tub to unlock the window. "And bring my bag."

Quick to follow, she was silent and trembling. Again, she avoided looking at him. And Frank was starting to get the feeling that his presence was making her uncomfortable. He knew he should say something to reassure her, but what? He'd never been any good at this romance stuff. So he put it off. He had more pressing issues at the moment, like keeping them alive. Distraction could get them dead.

He stuck his head out the window and looked down. "Piece of cake," he muttered. "You first."

He held out his hand.

Ignoring it, she climbed into the tub beside him. Difficult not to look at another person that close, because like it or not, she was forced to do it.

She was wearing her scientist's face. Or trying to. Oh, hell!

Frank grabbed the bag from her hands and flung it out the window. Then he gave her a quick, hard kiss. Though he was highly tempted to linger at her lips, he wasn't tempted enough to chance dying.

"C'mon. I'll give you a leg up."

He cradled his hands. Flushed and wide-eyed, she didn't argue this time, but gave him her knee and gripped the windowsill. He lifted her weight and she easily pulled her upper body out the window, giving him a tempting display of her rear. He steadied her as she hooked a knee on the ledge and pulled her other leg through. Then, half sitting, she let herself drop.

Seeing her land and pitch forward to her hands, Frank felt his pulse leap. "Are you all right?"

"Fine."

She rubbed the palms of her hands on her trousers and moved out of his way.

Even as Frank hiked himself up, he heard an engine slow out front. He forced himself through the opening, turning on a slight angle to accommodate his shoulders. Dropping to the ground effortlessly, he reached up to shut the window.

"Maybe we can fool him," he said softly, "make him think we left through the front door hours ago in the middle of the night."

He picked up his rucksack and slung it over one shoulder. Then he took C.J.'s arm and rushed her along the back of the motel.

"Isn't the ranch where we left the horses over that way?" she asked, glancing in the opposite direction.

"We're not going for the horses. They'll be safe enough until we can send someone to fetch them."

"You mean for us to walk?"

"Only for the moment."

He took her all the way around the motel and crossed in back of the vending machine area. A quick look assured him the Jeep was parked in front of the office. And that another of the truckers was gearing up to take off.

"Keep to the windbreak," he said, leading the way along a line of trees and bushes until he was even with the eighteen-wheeler. He set down his bag. "Wait here."

Then, confident that he couldn't be seen from the motel office, he approached the truck.

"Can I help you, son?" the grizzled man behind the wheel asked.

"My lady and I are looking for a ride. Our transportation broke down and we're stranded."

Which was true enough, Frank thought, giving the middle-aged, paunchy driver a quick once-over.

"Where you headin'?"

"Anywhere you are?"

"That'd be Billings."

"Good enough. If you don't mind, we'll ride with you up to the interstate. We're headed in the other direction."

"I can always use company." The man opened the cab door. "Climb aboard, then. This train's about to leave."

Frank signaled to C.J., who sprinted from the trees. He took his bag from her and let her climb up into the cab, after which he followed and pulled the door shut.

"I'm Frank and this is C.J.," he said.

"Norman."

As the trucker hauled out of the lot, Frank surreptitiously watched the motel, using the side-view mirror. A ring of what looked like passkeys hanging from his hand, the clerk exited the office and led a man wearing a Stetson and dark glasses in the direction of the honeymoon suite.

Frank couldn't have sworn the man was Gilad—he was too far away and the side mirror gave him a warped view—but there was something familiar about the stranger's stance and walk that made him glad for his caution.

THE LOCK MADE a scraping sound as the motel room door opened to reveal an empty room.

The clerk flicked the switches that turned on both cupid lamps and shed light on the unkempt and empty bed. "Uh-oh, looks like they left already."

"What about the horses? They would have ridden into town on horseback."

"Don't know about that." The clerk punched at the glasses that always seemed to be slipping down his nose. "They were on foot when they got here."

"Any stables around here?"

"Nope, but there's Marvin Pritchard's place at the other end of town. Listen, my shift is almost up."

"And I thank you for your trouble."

A twenty dollar bill changed hands.

"No trouble." The clerk smiled and showed off his buckteeth. "No trouble at all."

They walked back to the Jeep. The clerk waved and went inside the office, even as one of the truckers staying at the motel left his room, came to an abrupt halt in the parking lot and dropped his bag as if in confusion.

A quick drive over to Pritchard's proved to be another dead end. The mares were peacefully grazing near the fence, so they'd either gone off on foot or hitchhiked a ride.

He took out his cell phone. Luckily, it worked right off.

"I missed them, maybe by no more than an hour or two. Round up a pilot for the helicopter and come get me."

WHILE NORMAN AND FRANK kept a conversation about sports going over her head, C.J. had trouble relaxing. She would be glad when they got to the interstate. The last sign had read five miles, so it wouldn't be long before they could get out of the confined space, thankfully. She wasn't sure which bothered her more—the man who'd made love to her now seemingly ignoring her or the driver covertly sneaking looks at her.

Surely a stranger couldn't tell that she'd lost her virginity the night before!

Then why was he so interested? she wondered, wishing she could edge closer to Frank.

Pride kept her from doing so. Since he'd so rudely awakened her—albeit with good cause—he hadn't had one soft word to say to her. And while it had produced the effect that he'd no doubt wanted—her ready co-operation—the kiss didn't count.

So she had to be content with the memories of one passionate night, just as she had promised herself she would be. Why did that not seem enough in the cold light of morning?

C.J. shifted in her seat and kicked whatever lay in the soft case between her feet and the gearbox. It felt heavy, as if made from metal.

"That in your way, little lady?" the driver asked.

"No, it's fine."

"'Cause I can put it behind the seat. Don't need it no more."

"We're almost there, are we not?" she asked, thinking they must be within a mile or so of the turnoff.

"Almost."

"Then there's no need to trouble you."

"You've already done that. Connolly there has exceeded my expectations."

Frank stiffened next to a confused C.J.

"I—I don't understand," she began, her pulse suddenly picking up.

Norman had called Frank by his last name, but they had only exchanged their Christian names. She glanced at Frank, whose expression was grim. Obviously he'd come to the same conclusion.

"You didn't really think you were going to get away from me, did you?" the driver asked, dropping what had been an affected speech pattern and accent.

She tried to bluff. "What do you mean?"

"Come now, Dr. Birch, you're too intelligent to play dumb. It's been a stimulating game but now the game is over."

"You're Gilad!"

Dear heaven, they'd played right into his hands once more. But how had this happened? How had he found them? How had they not seen through his latest disguise?

"So you know my name."

He didn't sound happy at that.

Frank touched her and nodded toward the door, and C.J. fought a growing sense of panic. Surely he didn't mean to jump out, not with the truck shooting down the highway at sixty miles an hour. She glanced up to see a sign indicating the turnoff was coming up in a mile—in about a minute. No doubt he meant for them to take advantage of the driver having to slow down, perhaps stop.

To keep Gilad from realizing what Frank was about to do, she asked, "How did you find us?"

Gilad laughed. "You've hooked yourself up with an inept government agent, Dr. Birch. You're lucky you're still alive. Connolly's good at getting women killed."

Frank went stone-faced at the accusation.

Getting women killed...

A horrified C.J. knew of only one woman. Why did this mercenary care about Irina?

"Nothing to say for yourself, Connolly?"

"I loved her, Gilad," Frank returned, adding, "I did love your sister."

Gilad—the brother Irina had counted on to help free Frank, C.J. realized.

"Then you shouldn't have endangered her! You should have waited for my arrival!" Gilad shifted down, slowing the eighteen-wheeler. "One more day. That's all the longer you had to wait, you officious American bastard—one more day and she would still be alive!"

The truck was shifting down to a slower speed. Heart pounding, C.J. watched Frank indirectly. His fingers were curving over the door latch.

"I would have given my life for Irina, if I could have," he said quietly.

"Don't worry, you still can. And you will!"

C.J. sensed the moment before Frank cried "Now!" He threw open the door and tugged at C.J.'s right arm, while Gilad clamped onto the left with a fist of steel.

"Oh, no, you don't!"

Frank was half hanging out the door, the rucksack dragging him down, and C.J. felt as if she might be ripped in two. But how to make Gilad free her? She used the only weapon in her arsenal—her wits.

She screamed, "Oh, my God, watch out!" as if they were about to crash.

A second of inattention on Gilad's part was all it took for her to wrest her arm free. Frank's weight dragged her down on top of him. Luckily some thick brush softened their fall.

"Let's get out of here!"

He grabbed up the bag with one hand and her with the other and flew across the highway as the truck ground to a halt. C.J. heard the driver's door flying open and Gilad yelling after them.

"I'll hunt you down like the dog you are, Connolly!"

Glancing over her shoulder, she saw the mercenary pull a rifle from the truck. Then she tripped over her own feet and went down to her knees. Only Frank's grip on her arm softened the impact.

"Careful," he growled, pulling her upright.

They were traversing a stand of conifers and running blind before a shot rang out. Its whine through the nearby trees scraped up her spine. Too close for her comfort. Frank pushed her faster until she couldn't run any farther.

She fell against him, gripping his arm and gasping for breath. "Can't...go..."

Frank nodded and stopped. He turned to watch for

Gilad through the trees. His chest rose and fell as if with great effort.

Which reminded her of the way they rose and fell together the night before.

Suddenly C.J. couldn't look at him anymore.

"A plan...a plan..." he muttered as he paced. "Irina's brother! Damn, why did it have to be him? Of all the mercenaries in this world..."

Yes, a plan, C.J. thought. She needed to figure out how to save Frank. Irina's brother, indeed. The woman he had loved died because of him. Knowing Frank as she did, she was certain that put him at the disadvantage. He was so honorable, so dedicated to her memory that he would hesitate harming Irina's brother, much less kill him.

And as much as she hated the thought of anyone having to die, it might come to a life-or-death struggle. Gilad was out for blood.

So if she didn't come up with a plan, Gilad would take Frank's life in trade for that of his sister's.

The mercenary would kill the man she loved....

Dear heaven, there it was, the very thing about which she had been trying to avoid thinking.

She was in love with Frank Connolly.

How had this happened? How had she bound herself to a man who either would die or go on to another woman, one whom he could love? Either way she lost.

How had she allowed her heart to be so vulnerable after so many years of protecting herself from the tragedy of her childhood?

"We have to get you someplace safe," Frank said. "Someplace I can leave you while I set up an ambush...."

He was talking more to himself than to her.

Her own mind whirling, C.J. went with him as he led her, more slowly this time, along a rocky incline. Gilad was behind them, tracking them, waiting for his opportunity. Maybe their route would fool him. No footprints in rocks. Maybe they would be safe from the predator, after all.

Even as she tried to look at the positive, C.J. knew getting away from Gilad wouldn't be this easy. He'd found them time and again. And he was motivated by more than money. Revenge was the strongest motivation next to love. Gilad wouldn't stop until he had it. Until Frank was dead and she was safely delivered to the Black Order.

The Black Order...

Her thoughts were whirling as Frank came to a sudden halt. She ran into him, quickly backing off as her own body flared to life at the contact.

"What?" she asked.

"Up there, on the ridge."

She followed the sweep of his arm. "A cabin?"

He nodded and started off again. "Come on. It looks like a hunting cabin, but it's not hunting season, so it's probably empty. You'll be safe hiding there."

"Me?" He was moving uphill so fast she practically had to run to catch up to him. "What about you?"

"I need to keep Gilad away from you," Frank said. "I need to stop him. I can circle back, come up around behind him and surprise him."

And then do what? she wondered.

If Frank didn't knock the man out on the first try, he would have to fight him. And considering who Gilad was, Frank would be vulnerable.

Approaching the cabin, she noted that it was indeed abandoned. And it looked as if it had been that way for many years. She followed Frank inside. Minimal shelter, nothing more. A couple of bunks without bedding. A table and two chairs. No windows, which, for a moment, made her wonder about any occupants, furry or otherwise.

Frank was digging through his rucksack, retrieving items and stuffing them in his pockets. He really meant to leave her and put himself in danger to protect her.

Because it was his job or because he hadn't been able to save Irina?

Panic rose in her throat, but she choked out, "Frank, I won't let you face Gilad alone!"

"It's the only way."

"It's too dangerous."

"That's a chance I'll have to take."

His voice had hardened, sending a chill through C.J. Could he do what needed to be done? she wondered. Or would his invisible walls crumble at another mention of Irina's name?

When he rose and appeared ready to go, she put a staying hand on his arm. "Don't, please," she begged. "Don't leave me alone."

"I have no choice."

He swept her into his arms and kissed her. Not the quick, hard kiss of the morning, one more substantial…yet still far too short.

"Stay in here, out of sight. I'll be back for you," he promised.

A promise he might not be able to keep.

Touching her lips, which still burned with his kiss, she watched Frank Connolly walk out of the cabin and out of her life. For logic told her this was it.

Either he would die at Gilad's hand, or…

Desperate to save him, C.J. dug through the magic

rucksack, praying to find something of use. She couldn't just sit and wait and do nothing.

She could endure losing Frank if he were alive.

What she couldn't endure was letting him sacrifice himself for something that he hadn't been able to prevent happening in war-torn Bosnia.

Or knowing that he was the third person she'd loved and let die.

Chapter Sixteen

Gilad froze and stepped into the shadow of a ponderosa pine when he heard what sounded like crying nearby. A woman sobbing her heart out. And how many women would be wandering out in this square mile of wilderness?

Always cautious, he changed direction, gazing around him to make certain there were no surprises. He couldn't afford an ambush.

Then he saw her through the trees—Dr. Cecilia Jane Birch. The scientist had set herself down on a rock in the middle of a clearing and was bawling like a newborn. Even so, she managed to appear beautiful, her golden hair loose and tangled around her distraught features.

Undoubtedly she was alone because she'd been abandoned. He wouldn't put it past Connolly to be such a coward as to leave the woman behind, thinking it would save his hide.

Gilad peered around to make certain this wasn't a trap, that the pilot wasn't lying in wait for him. Nothing stirred but a lone bird soaring across the open space.

And the Birch woman's sob became a low wail that pierced the air.

Easy prey.

Before she could even stand and face him, he was upon her. "Well, Dr. Birch...unhappy, are you?"

She rose, trembling, and asked, "Y-you're not going to hurt me?"

He searched her tearstained features. "That depends on how cooperative you decide to be."

"I'm ready to cooperate. I am!" she insisted. "I've had enough. Frank Connolly has put me through days and days of misery in this godforsaken wilderness, and now he's left me here to die!"

"Now, why should I believe you?"

"Believe it! I couldn't keep up the pace and he told me that either I make a better effort, or I could stay here and face you." She hiccuped and continued. "I—I couldn't go on...so he did. He's afraid of you."

Gilad smiled inside. "As well he should be."

She looked around wildly. "And he's long gone. You'll never catch up with him now."

"I have more stamina than you give me credit for."

"But I don't," she said, sounding desperate. "If you drag me after him...please don't do that. Please get me back to civilization. I'm begging you. I'll cooperate, I promise. I'll even work for the Black Order."

Which was music to his ears.

Gilad considered his options.

If he wanted both Connolly and the Birch woman, he would have to drag her, and she would only slow him down. If he left her, she might be rescued by some rancher and delivered to the Quinlan Research Institute, late and a little worse for the wear, perhaps, but delivered. Then he would have to admit to professional defeat. Not good for his reputation. Added to which, there was no guarantee that he could easily catch up to Connolly. Some time ago, the transmitter had indicated the pilot was no longer on the move, which meant he'd abandoned his bag, so finding him out here, alone, would be more of a challenge than Gilad was up for at the moment.

But when he was better rested...

For now, it made sense to take that which was offered on a platter and finish the job on Connolly later. After all, he now knew where to find his sister's killer whenever it suited him.

Perhaps he should apply for a job as a wrangler on Lonesome Pony Ranch....

FRANK HAD BEEN CIRCLING around the area, hoping to come up behind Gilad when he heard a woman crying and knew it had to be C.J.

At first he was tempted to leave it alone. He had a job to do. He had to keep her safe.

But the heartbreaking sound echoed in his head. For all that she'd been through over the past several days, C.J. hadn't shed a single tear. So why now?

Careful to keep an eye out for the mercenary, he made his way back to her as fast as he could.

An invisible fist clenched his gut as he wondered what had happened to her. He feared she was hurt. And yet her weeping sounded more of the brokenhearted category....

Surely not because he'd left her. That had been for her safety. He hadn't wanted history to repeat itself, in truth. And what delight Gilad might have in taking her life in trade for his sister's.

Frank suddenly realized the sobbing had been replaced by the drone of voices. A man and a woman.

He concentrated. C.J. and Gilad! And they were on the move.

Cautiously, he followed, but it was several minutes before they were in his line of sight. Expecting to see Gilad muscling her along, he was startled to see her on her own. The mercenary wasn't touching her.

What the hell was wrong with her? Why hadn't she stayed hidden? And why did she seem to be going along with the mercenary voluntarily?

A furious Frank stayed just out of sight and hearing.

He couldn't believe that she would forsake her principles, not for anything.

Or would she?

Frank could think of only one reason—him.

Damn her for being so noble! He could have handled this. She could have stayed safe. Now he would have a hell of a time bringing Gilad down without her getting hurt.

C.J.'s ADRENALINE DRAINED from her as they approached the eighteen-wheeler. They'd made it! No Frank, thank heaven. He was safe.

Gilad helped her into the passenger seat. "Stay there."

"Where do you think I would go?" she asked, her voice resigned.

"Where I take you."

Another minute and he was in the driver's seat, starting the engine. But rather than putting the truck into gear and wheeling onto the interstate, Gilad picked up the CB microphone and made contact.

"This is Masqued Mercenary. I have the package."

Package? Is that what they thought of her? An item rather than a person?

"About time" came the voice from the CB. *"How soon will you deliver?"*

Gilad's "It won't be long now" was punctuated by the driver's door abruptly being ripped open and the mercenary being pulled out of his seat.

"Connolly!" Gilad yelled.

C.J. scrabbled over the gearshift into the driver's seat to gawk at the two men rolling on the ground. A curse nearly passed her lips.

Why, why, why?

"Masqued Mercenary, come in," said the other voice.

A very American voice, C.J. realized, having been certain the members of the Black Order were foreign.

Ignoring the radio, she clambered out of the truck on the driver's side, thinking to tell Frank to go away. But he wasn't going anywhere. He was locked in hand-to-hand combat with the mercenary. Both men were using a combination of street smarts and martial arts.

Even if Frank would listen, C.J. realized, wincing when he took a punch to the head, Gilad would probably whip out a gun and shoot him in the back.

Gun!

Frank rammed Gilad with his shoulder and the men went flying back to the ground.

Remembering the weapon she'd pulled from the rucksack, she fished it out of her trouser pocket. Her woe-is-me act had been so convincing that Gilad hadn't searched her.

"I don't want to kill you, Gilad!" Frank grunted as he kicked out from the hip.

Gilad caught Frank's foot, and in a test of strength twisted it around so Frank flipped over to his stomach.

"Don't worry, you won't. It's you who will die."

Which was C.J.'s worst fear.

"Stop now or I'll shoot!" she yelled.

Her stomach knotted at the thought of actually carrying through with the threat.

The mercenary glanced into the barrel of the flare gun. "That's not even real."

Taking advantage of his moment's inattention, Frank flattened Gilad and sat on his chest, pinning his arms to his sides. Frank's fist flashed up, knuckles poised and aimed at the other man's throat—a potential death blow—but he hesitated too long. With great strength, the mercenary raised his hips and flipped over backward.

And Frank went tumbling, the moment lost.

Exactly as C.J. had feared—Frank couldn't do it. He couldn't truly protect himself. She felt sick inside. That Frank couldn't harm Irina's brother put his own life in greater danger.

The men got to their feet and in a crouch, circled each other. Frank moved in with a roundhouse kick followed by a flying fist. Gilad blocked both, but Frank managed to get close. He hooked a heel behind the mercenary's leg and brought him back down.

"Give up, Gilad, you're over."

"Not yet, I'm not."

He pulled Frank down on top of him and rolled fast, so his greater weight now pinned Frank beneath him.

"This gun may not fire bullets." C.J. moved directly in front of Gilad so he could see it. "But it's effective, especially at this range."

"If you had the nerve to shoot me," he grit out as he encircled Frank's neck and squeezed, "you would have done so in the plane."

Choking, Frank tried to break his grip.

"Don't force my hand!" C.J. yelled.

He continued choking Frank, whose every effort to free himself was thwarted.

"Gilad, I'm warning you!"

He ignored her.

"Gilad!" she screamed, and then, when he still didn't respond to her threat, she squeezed the trigger.

The gun flashed and the next thing she knew, the flare caught him at the base of his throat, exactly where she'd aimed. "Aah!" He beat at the flames suddenly enveloping his head and chest.

The stink of burning flesh threatened C.J.'s stomach as Frank rolled out from under the man.

"Frank, are you all right?" she gasped, truly sickened at what she'd been forced to do.

Staring at Gilad, whose upper body and hair were burning, Frank shook his head. He flew at the mercenary one more time, then rolled Gilad facedown and smothered the flames.

A *whomp, whomp* overhead made her look up to see a helicopter filled with several men descending on them.

They were rescued.

A little late, C.J. thought bitterly, bending over to throw up.

THE NEXT MORNING, shortly after dawn, before anyone else arrived at the Quinlan Research Institute other than the security detail, C.J. settled into her new laboratory. All stainless steel and white, it was antiseptic. Civilized. Work gave her the only meaning in her life, so she might as well pour herself into her experiments as soon as possible.

She didn't want to think about the man she'd killed. Didn't want to think about the grueling hours afterward, when she'd relayed everything she knew to Daniel Austin in private.

Didn't want to think about Frank.

Once the helicopter with Daniel and the other agents had landed, he'd withdrawn. He'd hugged her and told her that it wasn't her fault, that Gilad had gotten what he'd deserved, what he'd asked for. Then they'd been inside the helicopter. He'd stared at her with a stricken expression, but he hadn't said another word.

And then she'd known.

Work. It was all she had left.

She was busy reading the reports on D-5 when the door behind her opened. "I'm busy," she said. "I need to concentrate, so I would appreciate some privacy."

"After we have tea."

She fumbled the reports and turned, wide-eyed, to see Frank in a clean and pressed shirt and trousers, carrying a tray with a teapot.

"Frank...I—I wasn't expecting you." The words tried to stick in her throat but she forced them out. "I thought the men outside were my guards."

"They are."

"Then why are you here?"

"To show you that I can, when the occasion calls for it, be civilized."

He set the tray before her and she noted both pot and mugs were decorated with wild horses. As was the dish filled with foil-wrapped chocolate candies. The pieces weren't as elegant as her dragon set, but they were beautiful in their own right.

"You're full of surprises," she murmured, her heart squeezing tight.

"As are you."

Their gazes met. His was so serious she looked away.

"I had to do it, Frank. Gilad didn't leave me a choice. I know that his being Irina's brother left you in a difficult spot."

Remembering made her tremble. She clasped her hands behind her back. The next thing she knew her arms were pinned at her sides, because Frank was holding her tight.

"I was furious when I saw you with him, trying to save me."

"I couldn't let him kill you."

"And I couldn't let him take you. I couldn't lose another woman I love."

The breath caught in her throat. Surely she was dreaming.

"You love me?" she choked out.

"That I do, Cecilia Jane Birch." He set her from him and cradled her face in his hands. "I can't say goodbye. I'll even learn to be as civilized as you want me to be."

"I want you exactly the way you are."

"Then, will you marry me?"

C.J. thought about her lifelong dreams of the perfect life partner—another scientist—and realized that's just what they were. Dreams. Frank was reality, and if she'd learned anything in the past week, it was that reality made her come alive. Frank was exactly what she needed.

But was she what he needed or was she merely a substitute for what he couldn't have?

"What about Irina? I can't compete with a dead woman."

"No competition. I loved Irina, but our circumstances drove us together."

"And that's different from us…how?"

"*You're* different. Unique. I love you for who *you*

are. I love the woman who wouldn't let me stuff her full of wild game because her heart was too tender to let me hunt. I love the woman who stood her ground and argued with me when she was ticked off. I love the woman who was ready to do anything to save my sorry hide.''

He kissed her then, tenderly, longingly. A kiss that lit up C.J. from the inside out. She bloomed under his touch. She had no choice, really.

''I'll marry you, Frank,'' she murmured against his lips.

He pulled away, grinning like a fool. ''Then let's not wait.''

''Life is too short.''

''I'd bet any hotel worth its salt in Vegas has a room with a heart-shaped bed. Perfect for a real honeymoon night. Maybe there'll even be mirrors on the ceiling. We can fly off to Vegas and be married today!''

C.J. laughed. ''Only if you promise *not* to fly the plane yourself!''

STANDING ON THE FRONT porch with the McMurtys, Daniel waved goodbye to Frank and C.J. as the SUV pulled away. Whitney was driving them to the airport.

''Sweeping her off to get married just like that. How romantic.'' Dale sighed and eyed her husband. ''Certain old men could learn a thing or two from that boy.''

''And how do you know someone older and wiser didn't advise him?''

Daniel slipped inside and left them to their good-natured wrangling. In the living area, Jewel was off brooding by herself. Her good mood at Frank's return hadn't lasted. He guessed she didn't approve of the upcoming nuptials.

Molly crawled onto the couch and into Jewel's lap.

"Want me to read you a story?" She held her picture book upside down and opened it. "That's what Daddy does when I'm sad and missing Mommy."

Jewel softened and put her arm around the little girl. "Sure, kid, I'd like that."

Watching them reminded him of Jessie. Daniel missed his son more than anything, and wondered if he could get his ex-wife to let the twelve-year-old come from Maryland alone for a visit. When things cooled down around here he would talk to Sherry about it. And later, he would call Jessie, just so he could hear his boy's voice.

But first, business.

He signaled to Kyle and Court, and they followed him through the office and down to the war room, where they gathered at the conference table.

"The thing that threw me about C.J.'s story," he began, "was her certainty that Gilad was contacting an American on the CB. Obviously no one in the Black Order. I'm afraid someone local *is* aiding the terrorists."

"Maybe Patrick was right about the local militia group and their leader, Joshua Neely," Kyle said. "Someone needs to infiltrate the Sons and Daughters of Montana to find out for sure."

"This is F.B.I. jurisdiction, so that would be me."

Court Brody had been raised in these parts, so he was a natural.

Kyle was scowling at the FBI man, as usual, but Daniel nodded.

"That it would."

You've read the first book of
MONTANA CONFIDENTIAL.

Now don't miss book two,
SPECIAL ASSIGNMENT: BABY
by Debra Webb

Available next month wherever
Harlequin Intrigues are sold.

For a special preview of
SPECIAL ASSIGNMENT: BABY,
Turn the page...
And let the excitement
and passion begin!

Prologue

"We're pleased to have you with us, Court." The man smiled, the kind of smile politicians used to get your vote. His voice was deep and disturbingly calm.

Careful to analyze every look, Court Brody grasped the hand Joshua Neely offered and shook it firmly. "I'm honored to be here, sir," he said with as much sincerity as he could marshal.

"My friends call me Joshua," the older man returned with an ease that was both confident and knowing. "And I think you and I are going to be friends." That smile again. "Raymond tells me that you're very interested in our beliefs."

"I am." Court resisted the urge to scrub his palm against his jeans when Neely released it. "I've been away for a long time. But now that I'm back home where I belong, I'd like to be a part of what your people are doing."

Neely nodded his understanding. "Raymond, take Court and show him around. We'll give him his official welcome at the rally tonight."

"Yes, sir, Joshua."

Grinning as if he'd just accomplished a major coup, Raymond ushered Court toward the nearest exit. On the stoop leading out of the enormous meeting hall, he paused and slapped Court on the shoulder.

"I knew he'd invite you to join us right away. I knew it," Raymond repeated, his tall, thin frame fairly vibrating with excitement. "That's why I wanted you to come today. We need more men like you, Court. We've got to fight if we're gonna bring this country back to what it should be."

Court recalled the crowd of men, women and children gathered in the meeting hall for Neely's speech. The hour-long monologue he'd just endured reminded him entirely too much of a Sunday morning fire-and-brimstone sermon. Only it was Saturday, and this place, with its security fence and armed guards, was no church. Yet, Joshua Neely certainly fit the bill of preacher. Court had a niggling feeling that the man was anything but godly. Tall and sporting just enough gray around the temples to look distinguished, Neely made an impressive picture. No wonder people around here were flocking to him as if he were the answer to the Second Coming.

"I appreciate you bringing me, Raymond." Court plowed his hand through his hair and settled his black Stetson into place, then shifted uncertainly, playing his part. "I've been back a couple of weeks already and haven't quite figured out what I want to do with myself."

That wacky grin split the other man's face again. "Whatever you're looking for, buddy, you'll find it right here." Raymond ushered Court down the steps, anxious to show him around. "Joshua provides us with everything we need, and all he asks in return is loyalty." He fixed Court with a you-know-what-I-mean look. "*Complete* loyalty."

Before Court could utter the response poised on the tip of his tongue, a tall figure, definitely female, rushed around the corner of the building and skidded to a stop directly in front of them. Raymond backed up a step to let the woman, who was clearly in a hell of a hurry, pass. Court surveyed her speculatively, then froze. His heart dropped all the way to his well-broken-in boots.

Sabrina.

For a full ten seconds all he could do was look at her. Still tall and thin, with a luscious mixture of car-amel-and-honey-colored hair falling around her shoulders, she stared right back at him. Those eyes—Court swallowed tightly—dark chocolate brown, wide with long lashes tipped in gold. Right now those gorgeous eyes were registering the same shock as Court's own no doubt were. God, it felt like a lifetime since he'd seen her.

"Court?"

His name was hardly more than a whisper on her full lips, but the sound was enough to snap him out of the trance he'd drifted into.

"What're you doing here?" A questioning frown pleated her smooth brow.

"Court's my new recruit," Raymond enthused before Court could fully gather his wits. "You know him, Sabrina?"

She knew him, all right. Adrenaline pounded through Court's veins. Sabrina Korbett was the only person in this godforsaken place that knew he was a special agent for the Federal Bureau of Investigation.

"Yes," she said, confused. "But I thought—"

"It's been a long time," Court interrupted smoothly as he grabbed her by the shoulders and jerked her against him. "Too long." Inclining his head to the right, his mouth closed over hers before she could fully comprehend his intent. She tensed, but in no time at all she surrendered to his kiss…just like before.

She was soft, and warm, and her mouth opened for his as if two years hadn't passed since they'd laid eyes on each other. As if…the past hadn't happened at all. He accepted her instinctive invitation, his tongue sliding along hers, his fingers automatically tightening around her slender arms. The same need that had always filled him when he so much as looked at Sabrina washed over him now, making him weak with want, making his blood boil in his veins.

"Guess you know each other pretty well. I'll… ah…just wait over by the training center," Raymond announced, breaking the fragile connection that had whisked Court back into the past he'd tried so hard to forget.

Sabrina flattened her palms against his chest, and tried to push him away. He knew he had to stop, but, *damn,* he didn't want to. The feel of her touch, even knowing that she was pushing him away, arced through him.

"Stop," she managed to blurt between his stolen kisses.

Court drew back just far enough to look into those wide, startled eyes. He focused his most intimidating glare down at her. "You don't know me anymore, Brin, so don't say anything we'll both regret."

She wrenched out of his grasp and glared back at him. Court knew the instant she'd made her decision. he braced himself for the blow.

Sabrina slapped him hard.

He deserved it.

"I don't know what you're doing back here, Court

Brody," she said hotly, her breath still ragged from his kiss. "And I don't care, but I want you to stay away from me."

Court held her gaze for two beats longer, as difficult as that proved with her glaring daggers at him and his lips yearning to mate with hers once more. "Just remember what I said, and we'll both be *safe*."

She blinked and uncertainty replaced some of the fury in her eyes. "Is...this some sort of undercover job?" Anxiety tightened the pretty features of her face. "You're not...are you here to—"

He forced a bitter laugh. "Hate to disappoint you, but I'm not that guy anymore. *You don't know me*."

He walked away without looking back. His heart skipped a beat or two as he struggled to calm his breathing. Raymond was waiting, probably wondering what was up with the little episode of "remember when" that Court and Sabrina had just played out. Now he'd have to figure out a way to explain that kiss.

Damn.

Just what he needed—he swore again—to get his cover made before he even got started with this assignment. Court blew out a breath as he strode in the direction of the training center. It never once entered his mind that he might run into her at this militia compound. Sabrina should be married and raising a family by now. Court clenched his jaw at the thought of her with another man.

She sure as hell didn't belong to him. And Sabrina Korbett was a distraction he didn't need right now. Especially not *here*.

Getting into the compound had been easy.

Now all he had to do was stay alive until he got the information he needed.

But Sabrina knew his secret. If she told anyone what she knew, all the information in the world wouldn't do Court any good.

Because he'd be a dead man.

*Harlequin truly does
make any time special. . . .
This year we are celebrating
weddings in style!*

A Walk Down the Aisle
WEDDING CELEBRATION

To help us celebrate, we want you to tell us how wearing the Harlequin wedding gown will make your wedding day special. As the grand prize, Harlequin will offer one lucky bride the chance to **"Walk Down the Aisle"** in the Harlequin wedding gown!

There's more...

For her honeymoon, she and her groom will spend five nights at the **Hyatt Regency Maui.** As part of this five-night honeymoon at the hotel renowned for its romantic attractions, the couple will enjoy a candlelit dinner for two in Swan Court, a sunset sail on the hotel's catamaran, and duet spa treatments.

Maui • Molokai • Lanai

To enter, please write, in, 250 words or less, how wearing the Harlequin wedding gown will make your wedding day special. The entry will be judged based on its emotionally compelling nature, its originality and creativity, and its sincerity. This contest is open to Canadian and U.S. residents only and to those who are 18 years of age and older. There is no purchase necessary to enter. Void where prohibited. See further contest rules attached. Please send your entry to:

Walk Down the Aisle Contest

In Canada	In U.S.A.
P.O. Box 637	P.O. Box 9076
Fort Erie, Ontario	3010 Walden Ave.
L2A 5X3	Buffalo, NY 14269-9076

You can also enter by visiting www.eHarlequin.com
Win the Harlequin wedding gown and the vacation of a lifetime!
The deadline for entries is October 1, 2001.

HARLEQUIN®
Makes any time special ®

PHWDACONT1

HARLEQUIN WALK DOWN THE AISLE TO MAUI CONTEST 1197
OFFICIAL RULES
NO PURCHASE NECESSARY TO ENTER

1. To enter, follow directions published in the offer to which you are responding. Contest begins April 2, 2001, and ends on October 1, 2001. Method of entry may vary. Mailed entries must be postmarked by October 1, 2001, and received by October 8, 2001.

2. Contest entry may be, at times, presented via the Internet, but will be restricted solely to residents of certain geographic areas that are disclosed on the Web site. To enter via the Internet, if permissible, access the Harlequin Web site (www.eHarlequin.com) and follow the directions displayed online. Online entries must be received by 11:59 p.m. E.S.T. on October 1, 2001.

   In lieu of submitting an entry online, enter by mail by hand-printing (or typing) on an 8½" x 11" plain piece of paper, your name, address (including zip code), Contest number/name and in 250 words or fewer, why winning a Harlequin wedding dress would make your wedding day special. Mail via first-class mail to: Harlequin Walk Down the Aisle Contest 1197, (in the U.S.) P.O. Box 9076, 3010 Walden Avenue, Buffalo, NY 14269-9076, (in Canada) P.O. Box 637, Fort Erie, Ontario L2A 5X3, Canada.

   Limit one entry per person, household address and e-mail address. Online and/or mailed entries received from persons residing in geographic areas in which Internet entry is not permissible will be disqualified.

3. Contests will be judged by a panel of members of the Harlequin editorial, marketing and public relations staff based on the following criteria:

   - Originality and Creativity—50%
   - Emotionally Compelling—25%
   - Sincerity—25%

   In the event of a tie, duplicate prizes will be awarded. Decisions of the judges are final.

4. All entries become the property of Torstar Corp. and will not be returned. No responsibility is assumed for lost, late, illegible, incomplete, inaccurate, nondelivered or misdirected mail or misdirected e-mail, for technical, hardware or software failures of any kind, lost or unavailable network connections, or failed, incomplete, garbled or delayed computer transmission or any human error which may occur in the receipt or processing of the entries in this Contest.

5. Contest open only to residents of the U.S. (except Puerto Rico) and Canada, who are 18 years of age or older, and is void wherever prohibited by law; all applicable laws and regulations apply. Any litigation within the Province of Quebec respecting the conduct or organization of a publicity contest may be submitted to the Régie des alcools, des courses et des jeux for a ruling. Any litigation respecting the awarding of a prize may be submitted to the Régie des alcools, des courses et des jeux only for the purpose of helping the parties reach a settlement. Employees and immediate family members of Torstar Corp. and D. L. Blair, Inc., their affiliates, subsidiaries and all other agencies, entities and persons connected with the use, marketing or conduct of this Contest are not eligible to enter. Taxes on prizes are the sole responsibility of winners. Acceptance of any prize offered constitutes permission to use winner's name, photograph or other likeness for the purposes of advertising, trade and promotion on behalf of Torstar Corp., its affiliates and subsidiaries without further compensation to the winner, unless prohibited by law.

6. Winners will be determined no later than November 15, 2001, and will be notified by mail. Winners will be required to sign and return an Affidavit of Eligibility form within 15 days after winner notification. Noncompliance within that time period may result in disqualification and an alternative winner may be selected. Winners of trip must execute a Release of Liability prior to ticketing and must possess required travel documents (e.g. passport, photo ID) where applicable. Trip must be completed by November 2002. No substitution of prize permitted by winner. Torstar Corp. and D. L. Blair, Inc., their parents, affiliates, and subsidiaries are not responsible for errors in printing or electronic presentation of Contest, entries and/or game pieces. In the event of printing or other errors which may result in unintended prize values or duplication of prizes, all affected game pieces or entries shall be null and void. If for any reason the Internet portion of the Contest is not capable of running as planned, including infection by computer virus, bugs, tampering, unauthorized intervention, fraud, technical failures, or any other causes beyond the control of Torstar Corp. which corrupt or affect the administration, secrecy, fairness, integrity or proper conduct of the Contest, Torstar Corp. reserves the right, at its sole discretion, to disqualify any individual who tampers with the entry process and to cancel, terminate, modify or suspend the Contest or the Internet portion thereof. In the event of a dispute regarding an online entry, the entry will be deemed submitted by the authorized holder of the e-mail account submitted at the time of entry. Authorized account holder is defined as the natural person who is assigned to an e-mail address by an Internet access provider, online service provider or other organization that is responsible for arranging e-mail address for the domain associated with the submitted e-mail address. **Purchase or acceptance of a product offer does not improve your chances of winning.**

7. Prizes: (1) Grand Prize—A Harlequin wedding dress (approximate retail value: $3,500) and a 5-night/6-day honeymoon trip to Maui, HI, including round-trip air transportation provided by Maui Visitors Bureau from Los Angeles International Airport (winner is responsible for transportation to and from Los Angeles International Airport) and a Harlequin Romance Package, including hotel accomodations (double occupancy) at the Hyatt Regency Maui Resort and Spa, dinner for (2) two at Swan Court, a sunset sail on Kiele V and a spa treatment for the winner (approximate retail value: $4,000); (5) Five runner-up prizes of a $1000 gift certificate to selected retail outlets to be determined by Sponsor (retail value $1000 ea.). Prizes consist of only those items listed as part of the prize. Limit one prize per person. All prizes are valued in U.S. currency.

8. For a list of winners (available after December 17, 2001) send a self-addressed, stamped envelope to: Harlequin Walk Down the Aisle Contest 1197 Winners, P.O. Box 4200 Blair, NE 68009-4200 or you may access the www.eHarlequin.com Web site through January 15, 2002.

Contest sponsored by Torstar Corp., P.O. Box 9042, Buffalo, NY 14269-9042, U.S.A.

PHWDACONT2